King of Sin

Hannah Pfeffer

Contents

Chapter 1

Angelique had always admired how city lit up in the night. Thousands of lights coming to life all at once to disturb the inevitable darkness.

This night was different. Way different.

Her stomach in knots, she nearly felt her lunch climbing back up her throat. Trembling fingers gripped the edges of her trench coat and her sea blue eyes were wide with terror.

'Royal Club' - Read a threateningly large neon sign above door leading to a basement. It's red light cast an odd glow on the bouncer standing underneath, making the bald man look ten times more scary. As if the tattoos and constantly squinted eyes weren't enough.

The poor blond haired girl standing across the street was ready to bend over the nearest trashcan at this point. She did not want to go there or be anywhere near the place, but the clock had already hit midnight five minutes ago, and she hardly had the choice.

Forcing her stiff legs to move, Angelique finally gathered enough courage to approach. She tried to look brave, keep her head high. Emphasis on tried. Her steps in the high heels were clumsy and her complexion had turned greenish.

She was terrified.

"Hello, My name is-"

"The back door." The guard grunted out without the second look at her.

"But..."

"The staff goes through the back door." He repeated, already sounding annoyed.

She hadn't expected a friendly welcome, but this was hardly encouraging. "Right. Thanks..."

First brick dropped on my head. Oh, dad...Why did we come to this?

There was only one reason, and one reason alone, why she had wind up questing for the right entrance into a strip club - Her father's addiction to gambling. It was bad, but she hadn't realized just how much until couple days ago, when she found him in middle of the living room, surrounded by three armed goons.

Apparently he's in debt to a very dangerous man, and of course, being the bad gambler he is, he's broke as a joke.

So there she was, scouting for the backdoor of some Russian club to repay his debt by dancing.

Five more minutes later she was finally let inside by another guard. The building wasn't much to tell a story about, but once the door opened, she was left awestruck. Red color dominated the surroundings, oozing luxury. Pictures of naked women were hanged along the walls, not allowing her to forget where she was for a second.

The interior was magnificent, and the least of her problems. When the guard lead her to changing room, she was greeted by ear-splitting voices of two women.

"Oh my God! I'm sweating like a pig!" The first one exclaimed, slumped into a chair near huge, brightly lit mirror.

"Duah. Cuz' you are one."

"Shut the fuck up, Zoe. I gained only two pounds and they're on my butt unlike yours."

"What are you trying to tell me, you fat-Oh." The angered woman, Zoe, cut herself off when she spotted Angelique awkwardly standing in the doorway. Her long, fake lashes fluttered, the green eyes hiding underneath scanning the newcomer from head to toe. "And who might you be?"

"My name is Angelique...I am the new...um...dancer." Her discomfort couldn't be hidden by any amount of bravery.

The girl sitting in the chair snorted, "Dancer, huh?"

"Don't mind that bitch." Zoe gave the other woman a mean look, her smile returning as soon as she looked back at the blond girl. "Here we don't avoid the word stripper, darling. It's what we do." She motioned to herself as if it was obvious.

And it was.

She was only wearing laced underwear with a transparent robe and pair of dagger heels. Her makeup looked heavy enough to fall right off her roundish face. There was hardly anything that didn't give away her profession. Even her dark red hair had glitter in them.

"Come on in, Jess is about to get off the stage and it won't be pretty if you stand in her way," The red head pulled Angelique inside the changing room. "By the way, my name is Zoe and that grumpy wench is Lila."

"I dare you to call me that again."

"Ignore her. She's on her period." Zoe said dismissively. "Angelique you said? That's cute, I think I have the perfect stage name for you."

Wow, that woman is bubbly.

"Stage name?" Angelique cocked her eyebrow. Why would anyone request her name in the first place?

"Duah. We don't use our real names. Do you know what bunch of stalkers come here? It's hard enough without them moaning out my real name when I grind on them."

This made Angelique cringe.

The door to the changing room swung open, "God, I will kill that old ballsack! So gross." Another woman stormed in, her dark tan skin glistening with sweat. Her blushed cheeks were puffed out in rage and her lips parted. "Some old dude groped my ass again." She fumed, pausing only when her eyes met Angelique's.

"Who's this?"

"Hey, Jess. This is our little Angel." Zeo introduced, smiling brightly.

"It's actually Angelique-"

"An Angel you say? This one looks like she fell from a driving truck instead of heaven. Is she going to perform today?" Jess frowned, her arms crossing right under her gigantic triple D sized cups.

Lila chuckled, "Agreed. If we let her out like this, Boss will cut off from all of us."

That's a little rude.

"I'm on it." Zoe suddenly grabbed Angelique by the shoulders. "We're going to give a makeover. Blonde hair will drive men wild, but the rest....hm...we'll work on it."

Before the young woman could protest she was pushed into one of the chairs. Zoe was quick to apply makeup and do her hair. By the time she was done, Angelique could barely recognize herself. She looked...older, sexier. The long lashes and wide black streak of eyeliner completely changed her features.

She didn't have much time to admire before she was pushed behind red curtain to change.

"Thank God I have some of my old bra's still here. Otherwise we wouldn't have anything to give you." Zoe shoved the underwear into Angelique's hand with two jelly-like things.

"Um? What are those?" The blonde questioned, holding one of them between her fingers.

"Jeez. That girl hasn't seen anything." Lila grumbled.

"It's for your boobs, darling. Put them into your bra." Zoe instructed, chuckling.

"Do I really have to? I mean.."

"Angel, no man is going to get an erection from a wobbling twig. Do it." Jess chimed in. "Just try not to lose them. Girl before you did, It was a scandal."

"That's not exactly calming." Angelique sighed, stuffing the pads under her bra. They felt strange. But even more uncomfortable were the thong. The thin strap didn't hide anything. At all.

"Isn't there a different underwear I can wear?"

"No! It's your first day! It's show or go!" Zoe ripped open the curtain, her red lips curled upwards. After a very brief moment of silence she nodded in approval. "You're set. Put on the shoes and let's go. The next show is about to start soon and I already told the DJ that an Angel will be coming up next."

The white lingerie she was given quite fit the act. Not that it mattered. Her stomach was already wretched by worry.

"You can dance, right?" Lila asked, preparing for her own act.

"They wouldn't hire someone who didn't." Zoe argued, looking annoyed by the black haired girl.

"I am a dancer. But not a...stripper." Angelique admitted, her eyes cast downwards. Modern dance didn't require showing bare butt to bunch of horny men or to wear ridiculous shoes. It required precision and passion for movement. She feared to imagine what her friends would think if they found out about this.

"Well, now you are a stripper, so suck it up." Lila scoffed, turning her attention back to doing her makeup.

"As I said, Ignore. Let's go." Zoe urged, having caught the glimpse of sadness in Angelique's blue eyes. "You know what I love about stripping?" She asked once the two were out of hearing range of other girls. "Once you're on that stage, you're not you."

"How does that work?" Angelique chuckled bitterly, swallowing the lump in the back of her throat. The walk was way shorter than she had hoped for. Zoe stopped in front of another door. Loud music was blasting from the speakers and boisterous roars of crowd could be heard all the way down the hall.

Zoe leaned in, whispering in her ear quietly, "Simple. Up there you're not Angelique. You're the Angel."

Chapter 2

2 days ago...

"Damn the practice was tough. How are you still so chipper? My legs are a fucking jelly." Amanda whined from the driver's seat, her hands clutching the wheel as if it would slip from her grasp any moment.

Angelique chuckled. "It wasn't that bad."

It never failed to amuse her how Amanda acted when she was hungry. And she was always hungry after practice. That girl was pretty much was a toddler in twenty year old woman's body.

"The competition is coming up in couple of weeks, we have to work harder than usual if we want to win."

"Ugh...Don't remind me." Amanda whined. "You just got extra hyped because you got to dance with that hottie Dale this time."

"Wh-Not true!" Angelique rejoined, her cheeks turning a shade of hot red. And that did not go past the brunette at the wheel.

Large Cheshire cat grin stretched onto her face. "Aha..Rig ht. I totally believe you. When are you gonna ask him out-"

"Don't even start!" She loved her friend, but Amanda could sometimes be terribly nosy.

I swear, she should've become a detective instead of attending Art school.

The two hit it off right away since the first semester in collage. They were on the same course and shared the dream of becoming a choreographer. Angelique didn't have any genuine friends in high school. Meeting Amanda was a lucky card she had wished for.

"Oh, come on. You have a crush on him since forever." Amanda pressed.

"It doesn't matter. You know I won't ask him out. He's way out of my...league..." Angelique's words trailed off when she spotted her house in distance.

"Huh? Did your dad got a new car?"

"Not that I know of."

A black SUV with tinted windows was parked in her driveway. She felt her heart drop.

Please don't let it be more trouble.

"Do you want me to come with you?" Amanda questioned when she stopped her red mini beetle in front of the SUV. Concern leaked through her words, and honestly Angelique didn't blame her. She knew about her father's...bad habit. And the imposing car didn't promise anything good.

"No. Don't worry about it." The girl managed a weak smile. "I'm sure it's just a guest I didn't know about."

Amanda's face screamed that she didn't buy it. But she also didn't question. "Alright. Call me if something happens. Okay?"

"It will be alright. I'll see you tomorrow." Angelique shut the door behind her, and drew in a deep breath.

Her nervous steps took her to the front door. It was open.

There was an uncomfortable tingle in her spine as she carefully entered the house; a standard two story building with plain interior and very creaky wooden floors. She knew every single plank, tiptoeing her way down the narrow hall-way.

"Time's up."

Her figure froze at the coarse male voice coming from the living room.

"Boss has been patient with you, but he wants his money back." Another voice added, this one owning a different tone of bad.

Unconsciously Angelique covered her mouth with her hand, trying her best to go unnoticed, she peeked around the corner.

Three bulky men clad in black stood around the beaten figure of her father. The glass coffee table was shattered and she could see clear specks of blood on the ground among chunks of glass. They had him kneeling down, shaking in fear.

"N-no! I-I will get the m-money! I swear! I just need more time-" Her father's plea was interrupted by a powerful punch to his jaw. It nearly sent him toppling onto the ground, his hand coming up to cradle his bruised face.

"I said; YOUR TIME IS UP!" The gangster roared, his yellowed teeth bared in rage. Every word came with a wheeze of smoke-abused voice."We gave you more than enough to pay off your debt. Now you're going to pay with your life." The man pulled out a gun that had been tucked behind his jacket, pointing it at her father's forehead.

Angelique saw his finger linger on the trigger, threatening to crumble her life right in front of her.

"No!" Her voice sounded through the room, all eyes instantly snapping in her direction. Her breath glitched in her lungs. In a flash she had given away her hiding spot and now came to deep-rooted dread.

"I thought there was no one else here." One of the gangsters glanced back down at her father. His mouth hang slack, mix of horror and shock twisting his face in an odd way. Clearly, her dad hadn't expected to see her. He had held a naive hope she would be home way later.

"D-don't hurt her. Please. She has nothing to with this." He begged, desperation growing by second.

"Boss won't like witnesses." The man holding the gun turned towards her. Single glance got her stumbling backwards in heart gripping fear.

"Pity to kill such a pretty thing." The second man commented.

"You don't have to!" Angelique swallowed the lump in her throat. "I-I can payoff that debt."

The armed goon threw his head back, wheezing in laughter. "Ha! Really? And how could you possibly pay off 100 000 grand?"

100 000!?

The sum sent her head spinning.

Oh my God! Dad! What the hell did you do!?

"P-please. I will find the money-" Her dad pleaded again, only to be silenced by a violent shove from the gangster standing behind him.

"Shut the fuck up, ol' man." He growled.

"I'm sorry, doll. His time is up and so is yours." Her heart halted as the gun was pointed at her. "Nothing personal. You're just in the wrong place at the wrong time."

In moments like these, mind comes to a stop. She saw the gun, the absolute terror on her father's face and her entire life flashing by in a fleeting second. Her lungs filled with air to the brim, her lips held ajar with no words coming out.

Wave of adrenaline hit her harder than a bettering ram, but she was no FBI agent to jump to the opportunity and save the day. She couldn't move to save her life. But there was something else she did...

"I will work for you." Angelique blurt out, her own brain yet to catch up with the meaning of her words.

The gangster with the gun paused, his finger seconds away from pressing the trigger. Intrigued, he gazed at the shaking woman. "Work for us? Aside from a good fuck, there's nothing you can give us, girl." He chuckled darkly. "I wouldn't say no to that though."

Angelique stumbled backwards when the man took a step closer to her. "P-please don't..." Her eyes widened, she hadn't even thought of the things they could do to her. Things worse than death.

"Wait." The third man who had been silent all this time spoke. He sat in the armchair, his legs crossed and a bored look plastered on his face. Somehow he was capable of giving her more chills than the guy with the gun did. His icy eyes rested on her as if they were capable of seeing right through her trembling figure.

"A girl recently...quit. Boss is looking for a new one." He stated calmly. There was an air of power about the man, he commanded the room without moving an inch. It was like the scene didn't bothering him the slightest. A bleeding man kneeling on the ground, a woman being threatened with a gun; he'd seen it all and more.

"She'll do for the job."

Present...

The velvety red curtain were pulled open, revealing a large hall bustling with life. The sort of beats that revved up the soul blasted through the speakers, driving the crowd nuts. Topless waitresses delivered drinks, giggling at clients that shamelessly touched them and couple more girls were lead-ing them off to the darkest parts of the club.

Air smelled of sex, nicotine and strong liquor.

"Good luck." Zoe murmured, pushing Angelique onto an ample stage with a pole.

The blonde hardly had time to react to the overwhelming scene before she was in center of a crowd's attention. A new beat came on and wild hollers echoed through the room, whistles and nasty words thrown at her from every direction.

Men, high on whatever concoction they had consumed yelled for her to strip and come closer. Her entire being was screaming for her the retreat to the backstage. There wasn't a single cell in her body that wasn't repelled by this.

But, escaping meant certain death for her father and possibly herself. On that faithful day she had signed her faith and now she just had to....

Suck it up.

With the first roll of her hips the mass of people below the stage went nuts. She tried not to look, to ignore the stretched out hands attempting to grasp her from the sides. In her mind, she was in an empty dance studio, practicing her routine for the competition.

Her moves sharp and precise, she approached the end of the stage. Her hips moved in rhythm and her hands ran across her body seductively. She had no clue how to work the pole, but she had seen enough movies and had enough experience in dance to try.

Angelique grasped the rather thick metallic rod, letting the momentum lead her body into a swirl.

"More!"

"I want to see your ass!"

"Come closer, Angel!"

Her eyes closed, her body twisted around the pole gracefully.

Ignore....ignore....igno-

Then she felt it. Steady eyes watching her from distance, different from those of horny patrons pushing past each other at her feet. This person's stare commanded her to look, way before she had her eyes set on him.

And she did.

Her gaze met two grey pools. They were like smoke blowing in the wind, coming from a fire that burned everything to the ground. The heat of his gaze could set her body on aflame.

Like a polished shard of metal it cut right through her, and her breath hitched.

Chapter 3

The feeling of being eyed up by a hungry tiger - that's how she could describe it.

His walnut brown hair slicked back, stubble covered jaw taunt, and impeccable suit on the powerful built...he stood out from the crowd. His head was tilted to the side slightly, hand caressing his chin in a thought while his eyes never left her dancing figure.

There was something about the man that gave her creeps. He looked dangerous as a stray bullet and handsome as a Greek God.

Two women sat on either side of him, desperate for his attention. One of them had her hand on his leg and the other was trying to kiss his neck.

He didn't seem to care though.

When Angelique finally tore her gaze from him, she had already lost her sense of rhythm, leaving quite a few patrons disappointed. She still felt him looking at her as she moved around the pole in an attempt to finish the number at least decently.

"Strip already!" One of the patron demanded, angered by the lack of show. She was already basically naked, but it simply wasn't enough.

Angelique disregarded the demand, twisting her body on the pole as the song came to an end. She wished for nothing more than to get off of the stage sooner.

But she couldn't help looking again. Her eyes trailed over the crowd towards the lounge. The man was talking to someone, his eyes no longer on the young dancer. Relief dropped over her shoulders.

He was unsettling, even more than the rowdy crowd.

She was quick to gather the money and disappear off the stage. It wasn't graceful nor seductive. The young woman literally ran off as fast as the stilettos allowed her to.

Zoe greeted her with somewhat a cringe on her face, masked by an awkward smile. "That was...Never mind. First times are always bad." She assured, trying her best not to offend. "But you did good with the pole, I actually was shocked. Perhaps we can still make something from you."

Angelique managed a wry smile. "I won't earn anything like that." There was roughly sixty bucks in her hand.

"Did you get distracted or somethin'?"

"Uhm. There was a man there..."

Zoe chuckled. "Honey, there are a lot of men here."

"No. He was different. He looked really...rich." She stammered, unsure how to describe the stranger with silver eyes.

"A lot of people here are rich. Mostly sons of wealthy daddies or the daddies themselves." The red head explained the obvious, giving the other woman a strange look. "It's your first day, don't stress. The money will come with lap dances."

That doesn't sound good...

"The show you put on there earns you clients. People will request you if they find you sexy. Simple." Zoe shrugged, marching back into the changing room.

Both women came to a stop. A short and rather bulky guy stood in middle of the room, waiting. He was engaged in a casual conversation with Jess before the narrowed eyes landed on the two women.

"Hey, Dog." Zoe greeted, her voice leaking hesitation.

This instantly put Angelique on edge. Was it normal for random men to show up at the changing room?

"Boss requested Angel." The 'Dog' said dully, he clearly didn't care for the half naked women in the room. His dark eyes zeroed in on the smaller girl cowering behind Zoe.

Angelique's heart begun to pump blood at the new speed. Her hands became clammy with sweat, and her complexion drained of color.

Was I that bad?

Dread coiled in her stomach. "W-what for?" She stammered, her voice broken by anxiety.

Zoe was first to catch up on her fear, "Dog, it's her first day-"

"I don't care. He wants to see her and he will see her." The man stated, silencing the woman. "Let's go."

The order rung loud and clear; she didn't have a choice. Angelique could only hang her head low and let the man lead her through the club.

For his short form, he walked fast, creating quite a bit of struggle for the poorly dressed girl in heels. She was lead inside a private lounge room. The same as the rest of the club, the walls were painted red, and a smaller stage was placed in the middle.

Ferocious eyes met her own. The same man who had observed her performance sat on a long half-moon shaped couch. His one arm was draped over a beautiful brunette and the other held a lit cigarette.

He took a long drag of nicotine, eyeing Angelique from head to toe.

"Nikolai, I thought you like your woman busty." The brunette at his side purred, pushing her boobs against his arm. The look in her eyes was poisonous. If it was up to her, Angelique would be bleeding on the ground.

But it was not. The man - Nikolai - had the power, and he didn't hesitate to use it.

"Shut your trap." He growled, eyes still on the blond girl.

The brunette yelped as she was roughly shoved to the side by the same arm she was snuggling against. He slowly stood up, imposing figure towering above everyone in the room. The suit jacket he had on earlier was now gone, the black shirt rolled up tightly around the bulging muscles of his arms.

"What's your name?" Smoke billowed from his thin lips with every brusque word.

Angelique quailed, clumsily stepping backwards when the distance between them shrunk.

We never give out our real names...

Zoe's advice bounced around in her head, all red flags raised high.

"A-angel."

"Your real name." He demanded.

"Angel." Her voice sounded like one of a cartoon character, high pitched and strained. Her cheeks felt feverishly hot, and her legs shook like branches in wind.

The man huffed the remaining smoke from his nose, small taunt smile stretching on his thin lips. He looked almost flawless, aside from an old, nasty scar across his left cheek.

"Angel..." He prolonged each letter like he was savoring the taste of that name. He came to stand close, looming over her petite figure. "I like that...Innocence..."

Nikolai's eyes trailed down her face, stopping at her chest. "Take off your bra."

The sudden command nearly got her choking on the air. "I won't do that." Her hands went up to cover her chest, which only amused the man further - if an ever-present frown could be called an amusement.

"Your father owns me a lot of money, doesn't he?"

So, this is the guy...

"I will pay you for everything you do. Take off your bra and I will give you 100 bucks. You will never earn enough by dancing on that stage."

Angelique gulped, her insides clenching. He patiently wait-ed, grey orbs drilling a hole in her. Like a deer caught in headlights, she felt frozen. There was something raw about the man. The way he carried himself alone made chills run down her spine.

The trembling fingers was a dead giveaway. She was intimidated.

The straps of the bra slipped down her shoulders, and shortly after the clasp came undone.

Oh, no! The boob pads!

As the piece of underwear fell to the ground, so did the jelly things Zoe made her put into her bra. She had completely forgotten about them. All her insecurities were writ large across her face, cheeks turning lobster red. For that solid second her attention was ripped from the man or her bare breasts. She stupidly stared at the two jelly things at her feet.

Mortified.

Like a call of hyena, the brunette's laughter echoed through the lounge. "Oh, God! How pathetic is that! The girl has even less on her than a plank!"

That hurt.

Angelique had always been skinny, but she wasn't completely flat either.

"Get out." Nikolai growled, not sparing a single glance at the other woman. Her laughter died down. She looked ready to murder Angelique, but didn't dare to speak against the man. With a murmured complain, she scrambled out from the room, high heels clacking against the tiled floor.

While she was glad that the bitchy girl was gone, a part of her almost preferred her there. Now there was just the two of them left.

He never touched her - he didn't have to. His unyielding grey eyes that scanned her naked upper body alone had her skin turning pink.

"Dance for me." He suddenly demanded, taking a step back to give her some space. "If you do well, I will double the money. And, don't cover herself."

Angelique's trembling hands slowly lowered from her bare chest. The chilly air kissed along her skin, making them perk. Shame swelled in her belly. Under his cold, observing gaze, she felt small and vulnerable.

She couldn't bring herself to look him in the eye as she climbed onto the small podium. Her small hands wrapped around the pole, pulling her body into the motion. There was no music. Heavy silence hung over the room, at times disturbed by the sound of her heels thumping against the stage.

Her moves were awkward. There was no rhythm to lead her other than the fast pounding of her heart. With the corner of her eye, she saw Nikolai leaning against the couch, his large arms crossed over the broad chest. He didn't look older than thirty, but there was hardly anything boyish about his features. They were dark; ones of a man that had seen hell and had come back friends with the devil.

He caught her looking. Nothing ever slipped past him, every subtle glance taken note of. There was nothing that could give away his intentions when he suddenly approached the stage, like a predator stalking it's prey.

Angelique stopped, her body raising from the impressive arch she had performed. Her baby blues clashed with his steel greys.

Her chest heaving with heavy breaths, she watched him produce dollar bills from his pocket. He didn't say anything, and his expression didn't give anything away either as he slipped the money into her panties.

Angelique gasped, feeling his fingers brush against her lower lips, lingering.

"Good." He murmured huskily, pulling his hand back a moment later. Like he had done nothing, Nikolai stepped back and took out another cigarette.

"You may go now." He said to the stunned woman.

She could still feel the sensation of his fingers as she scurried off the stage, money still in her underwear. Angelique didn't dare to look at him as she rushed out, his words ringing through her ears as the door closed behind her.

"We'll meet again...My Angel."

Chapter 4

"Awful! Angelique, point your toes!"

Beads of sweat poured on her brow, her back arching over Dale's arm in a graceful motion. The routine was tough and the sleepless night had drained her of energy. The silver eyes remained burned into her memory. Every time she closed her eyes, she saw the man watching her.

"No! No, no! Stop!" The teacher yelled across the dance studio, disappointment leaking from her jarring voice. "Everyone take a break until Angelique gets a grip of herself!"

The music stopped, bringing the dance to an awkward halt.

"Are you alright? You look tired." Amanda asked, eyebrows creased into a frown. "You're awfully silent as well. Did something happen at home?"

"No. I'm alright, just...bad sleep." Angelique wiped away the sweat, forced smile to stick on her plump lips.

"You know what you need?" There was an instant shift in her friend's voice. "Sex."

"Pff-" The sudden declaration nearly got her to spit out the water. "What? No-"

"You're a virgin for twenty years already. It's about time, besides...." Amanda's gaze trailed across the room. "Dale has been watching you."

Angelique resisted whipping her head around to look at the handsome light haired man. "Don't be silly..." Secretly, the thought made her all hot a giddy. She had imagined losing her virginity to him more than once. It would be all romantic and gentle.

But...

We'll meet again...my Angel.

His deep voice was still in her head. The predator-like charisma, the silver eyes, and the shredded body. Suddenly the picture in her head had changed. The man on top of her wasn't Dale, and he wasn't gentle.

She shook her head as if to physically try to get rid of the erotic thoughts.

"I want the moment to be right. Dunno, first time is..imp ortant." Angelique murmured, pink in the cheeks.

Amanda sighed, "I'm just saying....It will help you sleep at least."

The loud voice of their mentor cut through the conversation, inviting the students back to the dance floor. After the short break, it was even harder to be focused. Angelique constantly kept messing up until the class was over.

I can't believe I got scolded this bad...

The teacher was not happy with her performance. With competition this close, they couldn't afford mistakes. "If you want to keep your lead, get better, or I'll replace you." The old witch had said. She was strict and unforgiving, a retired dancer with lost fame - one of the best and worst out there.

"Don't be sad. You'll do better tomorrow." Amanda encouraged. "Wanna go grab some coffee?" She asked as the two sauntered out from the campus. It was extra busy today, people bustled around, their voices sounding throughout the school grounds.

"I don't really have spare money, I think I'll just go home for now."

"Come on, it's my treat."

Angelique sighed, hesitating. "Alright. But not for long, I want to get some sleep..."

I want to get some sleep before I have to strip myself naked in front of a horny crowd. I can't exactly say that...

Amanda cracked a lopsided grin. "Great. Cuz' I've been itching to tell you about this one guy-" Her garrulous friend carried on, overly hyped about some man she had met at a bar. Amanda was one of those people that didn't need much response when she got excited. She only required someone who would offer an occasional nod.

Religiously, Angelique followed the pattern, while her own thoughts trailed far off from casual girls talk.

Time passed by faster than she had hoped. These days she wished more than ever that an hour would turn into a year, anything to keep her from going to that god forsaken place. But, none of those prayers had response.

When the city sunk back into the darkness, she once again found herself by a dumpster, staring at the back entrance of the club. She didn't get much sleep, and no amount of make up could mask the bags underneath her eyes.

Her feet dragged, each step taking more and more effort as she made her way to the changing room. The familiar crowd was already there.

"Our Angel is here!" Zoe's chipper voice sounded though the room, her lips stretched into a wide grin. "Spill all the details!"

Puzzled expression crossed Angelique's features. "Of what?"

"Dog came in and said that the Boss wants to see you again. He never requests someone more than once. Tell us what you did." Jess added mischievously.

"Isn't it obvious. She's willing to suck her way to the top." Lila jeered, her sharp gaze never leaving the freshly painted nails.

"Get your fat ass up on the stage and quit talking shit." Zoe growled, "Now, Angel, give us some details!" The red head looked like a puppy expecting a bone, her big eyes sparkling with need for gossip.

"I...didn't do anything." Angelique trailed off, hating how her voice lacked the confidence and power. She was timid and unmistakably unsettled by the news.

What the hell does that man want from me?

Even in her own mind she was prisoner to those haunting silver eyes. The hurricane of thoughts brought her to edge of sanity. "Did he mention why I was....requested?"

"Nop. Why would he? Boss likes your pretty face 'is all." Jess shrugged. "I wouldn't worry too much though. He pays good, and...he's also the most chased-after bachelor that I know. Gotta admit, he's one hunky beast."

Zoe nodded in agreement, "True. But, be careful. I'm sure I don't ave to tell you what he really is."

Angelique shook her head. "I think I know."

He's a man capable of trapping souls.

A man with money and raw power. But that was not it. There was something darker about him. She felt it every time he laid eyes on her. His gaze held like a vice.

"Then you should also know that he doesn't like waiting. Go." Jess waved her off.

"Wait. I ain't letting her go with that hair." Zoe interrupted, swiftly hopping to her feet.

Angelique could only produce a muted protest before she once again was shoved into the chair. Fifteen minutes later, Zoe had done wanders, and hardly any sign of previously obvious exhaustion could be seen. She was send off towards the same lounge, wearing a different lacy underwear and the same stilettos.

Her knuckles rapped against the wooden door, nervousness building inside her. She expected her nerves to burst any moment, but every time she reached the highest point of stress, the bar raised. Idly, she wondered, how far she could go before she succumbed to fear.

A muted 'Come in' came from the other side of the door, the voice a familiar rumble. Gathering up what was left from her courage, Angelique entered, met by a slightly different sight from yesterday.

A table with two plates and wine glasses was set in middle of the lounge. There was no sight of the woman from yesterday. It was only the two of them, with her awkwardly standing in doorway and Nikolai sitting at the end of the table.

His steely gaze rested on her figure the second she took a step inside the room. The man was capable of devouring her with a single glance.He looked more casual than when she first saw him though, wearing a fitting black shirt with rolled up sleeves and matching color jeans. The light brown hair were styled messily, and yet still somewhat perfectly, giving him a more laid back feel.

"Take a seat." The invitation sounded more like an order as he jutted out his chin towards an empty chair across the table.

Hesitantly, she did as told. His gaze never wavered, observing every movement she made. She couldn't read what was going through his head, but she did notice his fingers curling and uncurling from a fist.

"Are you confused, Angel?" He sounded almost amused asking that, savoring the brewing tension.

"I am. Why did you ask me here, other than to dance?" Her voice trebled. She feared the answer.

"I want to have dinner with you." Nikolai shrugged his muscular shoulders, a taunt smile on his lips.

Angelique frowned, "It couldn't be that simple." Innocent dinner. Like hell. Something felt terribly off about this.

His smile grew into a grin. "True." A low chuckle vibrated from his chest. "I have a couple questions for you." He leaned forwards, muscles of his barrel arms bulging from his shirt. "Do you know how much your father owes me?"

The woman swallowed dryly. "I am aware."

"And you know what happens if you don't pay off the debt?"

"Not hard to guess." Her pulse picked up and fingers curled into her skin underneath the table. Her short nails left bright pink marks behind as she scratched the skin.

"You're a smart girl, aren't you?" Nikolai slumped back into the chair, breathing out a low chuckle. "No need to be so nervous. I won't do anything....yet."

Yet.

"I want to know more about you. Are you a student? Or do you have a job?"

The casual question took her off guard. "I'm a dance student." She answered with hesitation. She was yet to test the waters.

"Ironic, isn't it?" He didn't appear too surprised. "Do you enjoy it? You must have a lot of men chasing after you with that angelic face of yours."

Angelique let the nails dig deeper into her legs. "No. It's not true."

"Are you a virgin then?"

Her racing thoughts came to a sudden halt with the question. He didn't look phased, as if it was the most normal thing to ask.

"That's not really any of your concern."

His thick eyebrows furrowed, fingers once again curling into a taunt fist. "Just answer." His voice was calm, threateningly so. It left no place for disobedience.

The pressure between the two raised. Her lip trembled before she bit down on it. She didn't have a say in this.

"Yes....I am."

Nikolai looked satisfied, muscles relaxing somewhat. He regarded her with ease, letting the silence hang before he spoke up again. "Good...I want you to sell it to me."

"What?"

"Sell your virginity to me and I'll clear your father's debt."

Chapter 5

Her doe-like eyes were wide open and color drained from her flushed cheeks. The shock written across her face made his lips curl into a simper. His Angel was at the loss of words.

She demeaned him. Feared him. Her shoulders were tense with discomfort as she gazed at him. Nikolai was a patient man. He waited for those parted plump lips to finally give out an answer. He watched how they parted and closed with no sounds produced.

"No." Her voice was timid, quiet as a distant whisper. "No ...I won't do that." Angelique shook her head.

His fingers curled into a fist.

"You could pay off your father's debt in one night."

She shook her head as if it was the most horrendous thing she had heard. There was spark of something else behind her wary gaze, something he couldn't stand to witness in her eyes - defiance.

"I will dance for as long as it might take. I will pay off my dad's debt. But," She stood up harshly. "I won't sell myself to anyone." She wished her voice wouldn't tremble like it did when she looked into those silvery grey eyes.

A moment of silence befell the room. A thumb stroked the line of Nikolai's bottom lip, darkened wild gaze fixed upon the brave woman.

"Excuse me." Her golden locks swirled from her shoulders to her back. She turned and left without another word or glance at the man who still sat at the end of the table. Adrenaline made her legs move faster down the corridor, sound of her own raging heartbeat blocking noise of footsteps of behind her.

Short, bulky man appeared in the doorway moments after she had stormed out from the private lounge.

"Do you want me to bring her back?" Dog questioned, arms crossed over the barrel shaped chest.

"No." Nikolai's taunt tone and gaze alike exposed brutal nature buried under the handsome facade. The single word rung authority, one that young angel had dared to cross. Everyone here knew not to step on his toes, and she was ought to learn soon enough.

"Call Marina. I want to see her in my private chambers in thirty minutes. And arrange a special dance."

She had refused to go the easy way. Now he had no choice but to go the hard way.

"Whoo! That was far better than your first time!" Zoe cheered when Angelique had shambled off of the stage with roughly hundred bucks squished between her fingers. "Next time though, concentrate less on pointing your toes and more on climbing that pole and showing some ass." The busty red head wrapped a slender arm around her shoulders. "You got the crowd going nuts for you."

"That's not true. I still suck at this." The money in her hand hardly was enough. A week had passed since she first arrived at the club, and she had earned only couple hundred dollars. In this rate, it would take her years to pay off her father's debt. No amount of his apologies could be enough.

"As I said, more ass equals more money." Zoe chimed, "You might not have boobs, but you have a decent butt."

"Ouch."

She had grown used to the comments by now. Lila's jabs nor Zoe's friendly yet insensitive comments could be compared to the things shouted at her when she was out there, exposed dozens of groping hands.

"Fucking finally. Took you long enough. At least new thing warmed up the crowd for the real show." Lila's jarring voice echoed through the changing room the second the two other women had entered.

Zoe rolled her eyes. "Haven't gotten your dose, Lil? I'm running out of excuses for your bitchiness."

"I dare you to say that again." The black head snarled.

Angelique shook her head, disregarding the cat fight happening in the background as her fingers flipped through the cash. She slumped into the near by chair with a long sigh. Every night she climbed onto that stage, her eyes wandered off to the cushioned love seats at the second floor, but for last couple of days Nikolai wasn't present.

A part of her was relieved.

Sell your virginity to me.

Her thoughts had been poisoned by those words. The second she let her guard down, they came spinning back to her with the image of him; image of those hungry eyes that stripped her bare with single glance.

Angelique shuddered, desperate to rid herself of the looming anxiety.

Ping!

A message lit up the screen of her beaten phone. It had survived a fall from third floor and still functioned somewhat, and she couldn't find the motivation to purchase a new one. Dale's name showed through the slightly cracked surface.

~ Hey! Amanda gave me your number. I was thinking we could practice the routine some more. Are you free next week to discuss this over coffee?

Now her heart was beating for an entirely different reason than fear. Was he asking her out? A small smile bloomed on her lips as she reached for her phone.

Her fingers froze inches from the device when the door to changing room swung open, revealing a guy she had come to know, and much rather saw walking away than coming.

"Hey Dog." Lila was quick to put on a gorgeous smile. "Is it me?" If she would have a tail it would be wagging. "Please tell me it's some rich dude."

"It's not you. It's Angel." He grunted, narrowed eyes settling onto the blonde cowering in the corner.

Angelique felt her heart drop to her bowels. "Who is it?" Her voice fell apart into something unpleasant sounding as a single thought haunted her busy mind.

Is it Nikolai?

Dog ignored her question. "You have fifteen minutes," Was all he said before disappearing back behind wooden door.

"Congrats, your first lap dance." Zoe's lips twisted into a wry smile. The mix of pity and kindness was hardly reassuring.

"Of course it's her." Lila snorted, giving Angelique a killer worthy look. "Break a leg." The venom in her voice was perpetual. With a dramatic flip of her long hair, she turned towards mirror to apply jungle red lipstick to the plump lips. That woman truly was Miss Kindness. There was no doubt that by 'break a leg' she meant it literally.

"Want help with your hair? I'm up next, but I still have time." Zoe spoke gently, slight concern playing through her words.

"No, um..." Angelique sucked in a deep breath. "I'll be going."

"Wait, Angel." Zoe caught her arm. "Don't forget what I told you about lap dances."

"More ass?"

The red head bust out laughing. "Yes, that too, but I meant the money. The more you will do....the more you will earn." She smiled brightly. "Go get 'em tiger!"

It never fails to amaze me how she can be this optimistic all the time...

Angelique managed a quiet 'thanks'. With every step she took closer to one of private lounges, the bigger the coil of stress in her throat got. The bad feeling loomed over her head like a raincloud.

Dog opened door, inviting her inside a small room with a single chair set in the middle. A man in his late thirties sat comfortably on the chair, facing the door. "Ah! You're more beautiful up close than on that stage, Angel." He spoke the second she was showed inside the room.

Door clicked shut behind her and a shiver crawled under her skin. The stranger was eyeing her up from head to toe like piece of meat. His dark eyes reflected something that made her want to step back instead of approaching.

"Well? What are you waiting for?" He urged, shifting in his chair. She could already see a bulge forming between his widely spread legs. His hands clenched the edges of arm-rests impatiently. "I want what I payed for."

Don't be a coward....

Her hips fell into motion with beat coming from the speakers. Ignoring the deep sense of dread, she slowly approached. It took her every ounce of effort not to look away from the clearly turned on man in front of her. He was gobbling her up with his eyes in a way that made her insides twist with sick.

"That's right....Come here, baby." He breathed, disgusting smirk plastered on his face.

Angelique realized a second too late that she had walked straight into a trap. Once she was in front of him, his hands shot out, pulling her down into his lap.

"Let go! You're not supposed to touch me-"

"Fuck that. I can touch you all I want. I payed for you." He breathed against her neck. Every hair on her body stood on end. Lap dance was supposed to be a tease. Client wasn't supposed to touch the dancer.

"I will call the guards." Angelique threatened, trashing and turning to twist her body from his hold. "Let go-"

"Scream all you want, bitch. No one will help you. Did you really think, I will only watch you dance?" The man scoffed, his hands holding her tightly to his body. Suddenly she felt her breast being squeezed. "You're my slut now, and I will get what I fucking payed for."

Her eyes widened when his other hand begun to drag down her underwear.

"Now be a good girl, and shut the fuck up. You might enjoy this."

Chapter 6

Her dad might not be the pinnacle of fathers, but one thing he had done right. Taking his fifteen year old daughter to self defense classes. She hated it back then, and to be frank, never was too good at beating the blue man-shaped mannequin. But something did stick to her.

"Ouch! You fucking bitch!" The man roared when her knuckles slammed into his jaw with force that did more harm to her hand than his face. It did the trick though. The second his stubby hands released her to cradle his aching mug, Angelique shimmied out from his lap.

Clumsily, she pulled back. A gasp escaped past her lips when her heels got caught, sending her plummeting towards the carpeted floor. She landed with a painful 'thunk'.

"You will fucking pay for that, you slut!"

Her ankle was suddenly grasped, and her body dragged across the floor. "No!" Angelique clawed at the carpet, her blue eyes filling with tears.

"Come here." The man crawled on top of her, easily catching her thin wrists. "I will show you how to fucking hit me." He sat on her hips, rage tinting his dark gaze. She saw his yellowed teeth between the chapped lips that had formed into a hateful scowl.

"I wanted to go easy on you, but you're forcing my hand here." He whispered in her ear. His coarse whisky tongue licked at her skin. Tears were running down her cheeks in an uncontrolled stream. Her legs kicked and her body trashed against the floor, but nothing she did seemed to work. She felt his hand once again reach for her breasts.

Helplessness, disgust, fierce anger. She felt it all when his fingers slipped under the thin material of her bra, caressing the naked flesh underneath. He grunted with pleasure when her struggling stopped.

"Good girl. Stay still."

Angelique was shaking, her entire body having grown limp underneath him.

Is this how it's going to be? Will he rape me and leave me for dead? Is this really what's meant for me?

She looked up at the man as he moved back to reposition himself between her legs, the buckle of his belt already undone.

Fuck that.

"Aghhhhhhh!" His expression of lust and power twisted to one of pure agony as a tip of her heel dug into his crotch with all might the young woman could manage. The rapist howled out like a wolf in heat, now reduced to whimpering mess on the floor.

Angelique didn't stick around to witness him rocking back and forth on the ground and piss himself from the pain. With novice like grace, she got on her feet and rushed out from the room, panting and with tears wetting her cheeks.

Cool gaze of another man greeted her the second she left, making her halt abruptly. Dog was leaning against the wall across the hallway, calmly watching the scene unfold with cold eyes. He didn't say a word nor did he move as he glanced behind her at the mess of the man curled up on the ground. For the first time since she begun to work, she saw something akin to emotion on his rock hard face - surprise.

A part of her wanted to yell why he didn't stop the man, but all that came out from her parted lips was a sob.

Angelique hung her head low and rushed down the hall-way back to the changing rooms as fast as her shaky legs could carry her.

"Angel! What the hell happened!?" Zoe exclaimed when Angelique pushed past her. "Angel, wait!" The red head didn't waste any time going after the shaken woman, just barely managing to block the bathroom door being nearly slammed into her face.

Zoe found Angelique sitting on the cold white tiles, curled up in a ball with her face hidden by chunks of messy blond hair. Her shoulders were shaking with violent sobs.

"Angel..." Softly, the red head closed the door behind them and sat down besides her. "What happened?"

"I can't take this anymore....I can't! H-he....-sob-....he almo st..."

No more needed to be said. Zoe pulled Angelique against her side, hugging her close. "Shh....That must've been terri ble.." She let the younger woman cry and seek comfort. "We all have been through that. First time is always the worst." She spoke gently. Her usually cheerful tone was serious and understanding.

"I can't do this anymore." Angelique whispered against Zoe's shoulder, her breath hitching. Her eyes were puffy and red from crying, and she showed no signs of calming down.

"Why did you come here, Angelique?" The question was spoken with genuine concern. "You're not one of those girls seeking easy money, so why are you here?"

"My father's debt." She choked out, "He borrowed a large sum from....from Nikolai. They would've killed him if I....If I didn't come here."

Zoe inhaled sharply. "Jesus..."

"You have to help me. Zoe, I can't do this. I need to get out." Angelique lifted her head to look her in the eyes. "I am not like you. I can't stand this-"

"And you think I can?" The red head frowned. "You think my dream was to become a stripper for Russian mafia?"

"That's not what I..."

"No, that is what you meant." Zoe stood up. "You think you're the only victim here, huh? Grow up. We are all trapped, and there is no way out. Never." Her voice sounded cold, and filled with hurt. "There is no free ticket to normal life. Get cleaned up."

"Zoe-"

The door shut behind her with a bang. Angelique was left sitting on cold tiles with her tear ridden face red. "Shit.... shit....SHIT!" Her trembling fingers clenched the loose curls around her face. She felt her vision go blurry again.

Another wave of sobs shook her frame. "Why me..."

Sell your virginity to me.

In midst of hysteria, the same words had come straight back to her. Maybe there was a way out.

I'll clear your father's debt.

Slowly her head lifted from her lap. One night, and they would leave her family alone. She just had to accept.

Angelique wiped the fresh tears from her cheeks, forcing herself to stand back up. Her heart was ramming inside her rib cage. The young woman didn't bother to look in the mirror - she knew she was a walking mess and took no time to fix that.

All eyes turned to her when she exited the bathroom. Even Lila didn't dare to say anything. Zoe simply glanced her way, but remained silent as the blonde approached her.

"I'm sorry." Angelique spoke softly. "I know a way out, and I promise, I will find a way out for you as well."

"Angel....what are you doing..." Instead of anger, Zoe's face was of pure concern. She knew Angelique would do something stupid, but she had also never seen her this determined. "Where are you going?"

"I need to find Dog." Angelique grabbed a robe from the hanger and left the changing room in hurry.

She found Dog amongst the moving bodies of patrons, sitting at the bar with single glass of whiskey in hand. He was observing the crowd with steady, cold eyes. The man oozed stoicism, his pale blues spotted Angelique the second she walked out, but he didn't move a muscle to help her through the grinding bodies and grabbing hands.

"I want to see Nikolai." Angelique stated the second she had reached the bar.

Dog looked her up and down, taking another sip from his drink. "He's not here."

"Then take me to him."

"He is the one requesting meetings, not other way around."

"He proposed a deal. I want to accept it. Take me to him." Angelique demanded. "Please."

The man didn't say a word, simply staring at her over the rim of his glass. Finally, he sighed. "Get dressed. You have ten minutes."

Chapter 7

Thump Thump Thump

Her heart droned in her ears louder than the roaring engine of the black Mercedes. Its windows were tinted black, and fine leather felt like ice against her skin. That was nothing compared to the discomfort she felt when Dog ordered her to put on a blindfold. "Precaution", he had said. Wherever they were going, she wasn't supposed to see the road.

This made for the worst car ride she had been on, including the time her dad crashed into a tree when she was five. No radio, no conversations, just suspense.

Her breath hitched when she felt the vehicle come to a smooth stop. They had been driving on a gravel road for about fifteen minutes. The ride was long as well. Wherever this was, they no longer were in the city.

The passenger side door opened. "You can take that off." Dog spoke, already making his way further away from the car.

When Angelique removed the black cloth from her eyes, her jaw dropped. The car was parked in front of curved stairs leading up to enormous mansion. The kind you'd see in movies. Painted polar white, intimidating facade loomed over anything else.

It had this dangerous beauty about it. Even if she didn't know what it held within, it still had a vibe of a place you didn't just walk out of. Surveilence cameras were set on every corner, and distant barking of dogs guarding the perimeter rung through the night air.

"Are you coming?" Dog's voice snapped her back into reality.

Angelique hurriedly nodded. "Y-yeah." She hurried up the steps towards two large doors that lead into a luxurious lobby.

"Stay here. Don't touch anything and don't go anywhere. I don't have to explain what happens if you do."

She shook her head. "I got it."

And with that, Dog walked away, leaving her standing in middle of the gigantic room all alone. No more than fifteen minutes later, he returned with the same emotionless look on his face, and ordered her to follow along. If it wasn't for the simmering stress in pit of her stomach, she might've payed closer attention to the beautifully styled house.

The mansion was so big that she quickly lost all sense of direction. By the time they had reached the right door, she could no longer remember how to find the exit. Not that it would help her much if shit hit the fan.

Dog knocked, and moments later a deep voice came from the other side. "Come in."

Her insides clenched. The door slowly opened, revealing an ample office with a large mahogany table set in middle. Familiar, piercing silver eyes landed on her the second she took a step inside. Nikolai sat leaning into a leather chair, smoke of cigarette swirling from his lips.

He seized her up like a predator would it's innocent victim. "What a surprise. I wasn't expecting an Angel in my office." He didn't look surprised to see her, like he knew she would come to him sooner or later. The dark look in his eyes was unsettling. He didn't even blink as he stared at her through the billowing smoke.

Angelique swallowed back a lump that had formed in her throat. "I came to talk to you about....the offer." Her hands clenched at her sides, knuckles turning white. "Does it still stand?"

Nikolai took another moment to savor the quivering woman in front of him, and then slowly stood to his full height. The expensive suit jacket was straightened with a firm tug of his hand. It hugged around his muscular built, curving slightly over the defined biceps. This man didn't eat or drink himself to stupor. He was in peak shape.

Tauntingly slowly, he approached, taking a drag from his cigarette. The silver eyes never trailed away from Angelique. He came to stand directly in front of her. The smoke was exhaled directly in her face, making the poor woman cough.

The bite of nicotine had her wanting to step away, but he had her pinned with his gaze alone. His fingers came up to play with a loose curl of her golden hair. He twirled it around his finger before leaning down to inhale the scent of her shampoo.

Low groan rumbled in his chest, cold eyes boring into her own. "It does." He finally responded, releasing her hair. His voice had dropped to something threatening. It gave her chills.

"If I...accept...you will clear my father's debt? You will leave me and my family alone?" Angelique forced herself to look him in the eyes.

"Yes. If you sell your virginity to me, I will."

"How can I be sure?"

Nikolai suddenly caught her chin, tilting her head upwards, closer to his face. "If I promise something, I keep my word, Angel."

Angelique gulped, staring at his hardened features. "Then, I accept." The struggle to get those words past her lips was more than she had anticipated. She didn't want to sell herself. Just couple of days ago, she was so sure that she would never make such decision. And yet...there she was.

A small smirk appeared on his lips. "Good choice." Nikolai leaned in, his lips inches from her own. "My Angel..."

Her eyes squeezed shut, waiting for his hands to grab her, but instead he stepped back.

Huh?

Nikolai went back to his desk, putting out the remains of burning cigarette. "We won't do it here." He glanced back at her, "First time has to be special."

Her heart pounded harder in her chest.

"Meet me at Hotel Royale on Saturday. 8 pm, sharp." He sat back down at his desk. "And don't be late, or the deal is off, and I will double the money your father owes me."

"Spill it."

"Spill what?"

"What is going on with you?" Amanda had been trying all day long to catch up to Angelique, and finally had managed to get a word in.

"What do you mean?"

"Oh, don't you dare. You know what I mean. You've been depressed lately. You look tired and don't talk to me like you used to. Damn, you didn't even respond to my texts yesterday." Her voice quickly changed from annoyance to genuine concern. "What is going on with you? You know, you can tell me everything."

Angelique came to stop in middle of the hallway. She hadn't slept all night and the practice had her drained. And she also had to meet Nikolai that night. It felt like the world was weighing down on her shoulders. "You're just imagining things. I've just been tired lately. Don't know why." It was a lame lie, she knew it. "I just need some rest."

I can't just say 'Hey, I'm about to sell my virginity to a mob boss because my poor excuse of a father is a gambler.'

Amanda's eyes narrowed suspiciously. "Fine." She huffed, "Don't tell me." Dramatically she crossed her arms over her chest. There was a tint of sadness in her eyes. "I though we could talk about everything, but I guess I was wrong. Don't get me wrong, I'm not mad, I just want my cheerful friend back."

Angelique's jaw clenched. It was damn near impossible to hold the tears in, but she couldn't involve her friend. God knows what that man was capable of.

"Hey!" A honeyed male voice came from behind her, before her brain had managed to come up with a response she would consider good enough. Angelique whipped around in hurry, coming face to face with Dale's sunny features.

"I was hoping to meet you. You didn't respond to my text. I was getting worried." Wide yet somewhat nervous smile played across his lips. If there was a Prince Charming, it was Dale. Kind, gentle and handsome. He had all the qualities you could wish for in a man.

"Text message? Oh- That message!" Angelique stammered, feeling herself grow bright red. "Yeah, sorry, I was busy."

"Well? What's your answer then? Perhaps we could grab some coffee today."

Damn. Why does his smile has to be so adorable?

"I can't. I have....things to take care of. It's going to take me a while." The young woman pushed back the bitterness in her voice.

"Oh." Dale's face fell in disappointment. "Alright then."

"But I'm free next week. Monday maybe?" She quickly added. This night would be a nightmare, but after that she was free again. She could go out with a guy she liked...

The smile was quick to return on his sunny face. "Great! Monday it is. Let's meet after classes." Dale waved his good-bye, taking one last look at Angelique before walking off.

He even looks good from behind...

"Well, well, well...." Amanda's previous scowl was now replaced by a large Cheshire grin. "Did someone just land a date?"

This time Angelique let a small smile slip. "It's not like that. We just want to discuss practicing the routine."

"Suuuuureee. What routine are we talking exactly? Usually in bed it's a bad thing, but I wouldn't mind with him." Amanda nudged her side with an elbow, knowing look plastered on her face.

"Stop it. It's not like that." Angelique grinned, her cheeks rosy. She had dreamed about Dale since day one. This was the first time he had ever asked her out, and she didn't want to get her hopes up high only to be dumped. Though, a part of her was squealing in joy until....

Ping!

A message from an unknown number served as a simple reminder.

~ Hotel Royale. 8 pm. Don't be late.

Chapter 8

It was like taking a step into a whole different world. The second she got out from the cab, she found herself surrounded by classy luxury meant for those of wealth and power. Nikolai was both; she supposed.

This was the chocolate on the pillow type of hotel. A single night could make her broke for life. Angelique couldn't help feeling out of place. Her cherry red dress looked cheap in comparison of silk, shiny jewels and fur coats some women proudly wore around their shoulders.

Nervously, she adjusted her jacket, slowly making her way further down the impressive lobby.

"Miss Ryans?" Before she had even managed to reach the front desk, a man in a black suit with name tag that read Joel, came up to her.

"Y-yes?" Angelique cleared her throat, slightly startled by her name suddenly being spoken by a total stranger.

Joel smiled a picture perfect, and absolutely fake smile. His teeth looked whitened just for the purpose of giving those to please snobby clients. "Mr. Ivanov is expecting you. Please follow me." He didn't wait for her response. He hardly cared for it. Joel simply walked off towards elevators.

Angelique quickly caught up, her high heels clacking against the marble floor. An entire awkward elevator ride later, Joel once again gave her that creepy smile. "Room 785." With a stiff motion of his arm, he showed her out from the lift. The fake smile fell the second she had stepped into the hallway.

The young woman breathed a quiet sigh, her eyes skimming over the number plates on the door.

785...785....

Finally she spotted the correct door, and her steps halted.

This is it...

Her stiff fingers clenched the edge of her dress tightly to stop her hands from shaking. This was not how she had imagined her first time being. Perhaps it was naive, but she had hoped it would be romantic, and with a man she had feelings for. Never in million years she could've imagined that her virginity would be sold to a mob boss.

Her lungs filled to brim with air. She held her breath and rammed her knuckled against the wooden door.

There was a pause that seemed to last an entirety.

Wrong room? He did say 785....

As confusion begun to seep into her features, the door opened. "7.57 pm. You did smart not to be late, Angel." Nikolai stood in the doorway, for the first time dressed casually. He wore a plain black t-shirt and matching color jeans. His muscular, tattooed arms settled against his sides, somehow adding to his intimidating yet handsome appearance.

"I don't like being late." She responded timidly. Why the hell every time she looked into those intense eyes her knees went weak?

Something akin to lopsided grin appeared on his thin lips. Nikolai stepped out of the way, silently inviting her inside the suite. Needless to say it was just as luxurious as the hotel. Her eyes lingered on the large king size bed.

The whole room felt as if it should belong to a king. The violet rug looked as if it were brought to life by the finest threads, and the very walls seemed to bleed gold. Angelique once again felt the lump of fear forming in her gut. She could hear his footsteps slowly approaching her from behind, but she didn't dare to look.

"Drink." A glass of whiskey was presented to her. Nikolai had circled her, now blocking the bed from her view.

"I don't drink." Still, she took the glass.

"Tonight you will." Nikolai said simply. "It will help you relax."

Maybe drinking is a good idea after all.

Nikolai watched intensely as she took a sip from the amber liquid. It burned down her throat and left a tart aftertaste on her tongue. Angelique cringed, single hand raising to her lips as if it could cover her lack of experience with strong drinks. Usually her dad did the drinking for both of them.

"You're so innocent." He said lowly, fingers caressing her blond locks.

"Is that a good thing?" All her life she had doubted that. Perhaps she was too naive for this world, too easily trusted people. If she had more nerve maybe she wouldn't be in this situation in the first place.

"I like it." Nikolai took another step closer. His hand trailed from her hair to her cheek, down her jawline, "Makes me want to have you all to myself." His thumb ran across her bottom lip. "You're everything I'm not." His accent was thick, but he spoke fluent English. This was the first time she had noticed it in the first place.

A shaky breath tumbled past her lips. He was so close she could smell his cologne. The glass was suddenly removed from her hand and set on nearby table.

"I've never met someone like you. You're not dirty like the rest of them." Nikolai walked behind her. She felt his knuckles brush against the skin of her back as he unzipped her dress.

Her eyebrows furrowed. "Who is them?" The question came out before she could stop it.

"Women."

A feminist inside her wanted to scream, but the part responsible for survival made her stay silent. Her mind was quick to wander off to different matters when she felt a fierce tug on her dress. The fabric slid down her slender figure and fell to her feet, leaving her in nothing but her underwear.

Angelique gasped when the hook of her bra was undone with expertise. It soon joined her dress onto the ground.

"Don't cover yourself." Nikolai whispered the order in her ear, his hot breath caressing her skin. His breathing had grown rugged, mixing with low, lustful groans when his hands groped her exposed breasts. Nimble fingers toyed with hardened nipples, pinching, squeezing and circling the orbs with skillful motions.

Her eyes closed, uncontrolled intake of breath making her lips part. His hands moved from her breasts to her lower back, and she felt something warm and wet press against her mouth. He kissed her deeply, his tongue invading past her lips, stroking seductively against her own.

It wasn't her first kiss, but it sure felt like it. With their lips locked, his hands explored past her hips. Angelique flinched when his calloused hand grabbing at her tender behind. Her body responded with a flinch, which only seemed to make his satisfaction run deeper.

Nikolai pulled away from their kiss, removing his shirt in a fluid motion. His tattooed and scarred form now visible to the innocent woman. He had the body of a killer. His muscles were taut, mafia and prison tattoos covered every square inch of his body. Every tattoo carried a meaning. Some symbolized the lives he took, others told the story of a thief.

While some expressed love for his motherland, others spoke of slavery under and hatred for the government. His body served as a book of sorts - telling his story of fear, anger, imprisonment, freedom, violence, and death. The thick, jagged scar that seemed to sever his chest in two was but another reminder of his violent past, present, and future.

Angelique couldn't help her gaze wandering over the map of ink on his body. She had never met a person this heavily tattooed or scarred.

Soon her gaze returned back to his face, when he once again kissed her warm lips, trailing wet kisses down her jaw and neck. As a long, gliding kiss passed her collarbones, the world was suddenly flipped around. Before she could blink, Angelique found herself bouncing off of the soft mattress.

He had tossed her onto the bed without any effort. "You're gorgeous," He rasped, unzipping his fly and pulling off his black trousers and boxers. His spear was fully erect, it's mushroom shaped head glistening with precum.

It was said that first times hurt. Seeing his length quickly reminded her of the fact. She hadn't seen many dicks in her life, but knew that this one would hurt her badly. Angelique quivered, her fear of pain written across her face.

Nikolai sensed it. He mounted the girl, his lips returning to her neck and breasts, his fingers dancing at her thighs. "Calm down. It will be worse if you're tense."

That's hardly reassuring....

Nikolai traced his index finger across her thighs and to her clit. Aroused, he leered at her with hungry eyes.

Angelique's back arched with the sensation he had seeded within her. It was more demanding than anything she had ever felt. A breathy moan of pleasure tumbled past her lips as his fingers traced between the slightly moist folds. Her legs were kept apart by his broad body. Even if she tried to close them, his powerful built stopped her.

No one had touched her like this before.

He teased her. Kissing her breasts and gliding his finger across her most sensitive parts. she felt those first stirrings of lust. Both of his hands now grabbed hold of her thighs and pushed her legs farther apart. His toned body leaning over hers, his fingers now touched her with purpose. Bringing his index finger to her clit, he began pleasuring her.

While his intense gaze never lowered from her face, she couldn't bear to look at him when his fingers messaged her clit. Fairly quickly she felt the buildup. It hit her like a wave. At first it had been just a sensation and then it went through her entire body with sheer power. Uncontained sounds of pleasure left her lips and her form trembled beneath his.

Nikolai's finger slowed, still circling her clit until it became unbearable. "S-stop!" Angelique whined, her hips moving to escape him, only to be held down by a firm hand. "Please stop!"

He didn't stop until she begun to beg. Only then he moved his fingers from her clit, down her slit until they reached her entrance. Her body jolted when the first finger pushed past the tight walls and begun to move back and forth.

"You're tight." He grunted, leaning over her to kiss her neck. His finger buried itself inside her knuckle-deep, then retreated and suddenly another finger was joining the first.

"No. D-dont!" Angelique protested. What had been plea-sure, suddenly turned to discomfort. Her smaller hands pushed at his chest with all strength she could muster.

"Don't?" He shot back, her feeble push sending him a little more than an inch back. He stepped towards her again, closer this time. "You think you can escape this deal, Angel?"

He chuckled lowly, mocking her. "You are mine." The fingers pushed inside her far more forcefully. "You know you can't run away from this."

Angelique gasped with another fierce thrust.

"Either you let me prepare you, or I will shove inside and fuck you until you bleed."

Her eyes widened with fear. What had she gotten herself into!? Her shaky hands fell from his broad chest, now resting back onto the covers. All resistance was replaced by dread.

"Good girl." He murmured in her ear when she stopped resisting. His fingers begun to move more gently, pressing into her sensitive parts. His lips once again were kissing against her neck.

Nikolai shifted, his fingers retreating from her insides. His one arm came up besides her head, white the other took hold of his shaft. Angelique gasped when she felt the tip press against her entrance. Her thighs pressed against his hips, her hands shaking.

Nikolai leaned over her, his piercing grays meeting her baby blue orbs. "My angel." With a swift thrust, he entered her.

Angelique screamed as the next five minutes of hell begun. It burned unbearably. She clawed at his muscular back, even bit his shoulder to ease the pain as he pounded inside her with no mercy. Nikolai's groans of pleasure sounded in her ear. He was like a hungry wolf feasting on it's prey.

She clung onto his wide shoulders, all sense of time lost. Slowly, the pain eased away. It begun to mix with pleasure and his speed increased. His groans turned into lustful growls, and her whines turned into silent moans.

Nikolai lifted his head from the crook of her neck, planting a lingering kiss on her lips, pushing in even deeper. Her head lolled back as the building sensation returned. Her insides clenched around his pulsating shaft.

Few more thrusts later she was pushed over the edge. Powerful sensation spread from her lower regions throughout her entire body, making her soul quiver. Her lips parted, but no sound came out. Her body arched against his, every muscle tense, before she collapsed back onto the sheets, exhausted.

Nikolai wasn't done, however. His moves intensified to a near painful level. She felt him stiffen inside of her. Beast like growl rumbled through his chest as he suddenly pulled out, white semen squirting onto her flat stomach. He rubbed his shaft, grunting when the act was done.

Moment of silence followed. He stared down at her tired figure with cold eyes, and then got off of her.

"Your debt has been payed."

Chapter 9

Your debt has been payed.

Brutal. His unyielding silver eyes were burned into her memory. Even in her dreams she saw them gazing down at her coldly, she felt his callous hands pinning her down, his lips on her own....

The memory sent shivers down her spine. Nearly a week had passed since then, and yet she still couldn't escape from him. That man had invaded her mind.

"Are you listening?" A voice suddenly spoke across the table. Dale's slightly worried face came into sight when she lifted her gaze from cup of coffee she had been clenching in her hands.

"Yeah. I'm sorry," Angelique managed a weak smile. "I just have a lot on my mind."

Even on a date, I can't lock him out of my mind.

"Is it about the competition? You have nothing to worry about. You're an amazing dancer." Dale beamed. He reached across the table, gently taking her hand into his. "I actually can't wait to perform the dance with you." His voice was soft, flirty. The light haired school hottie was nothing like Nikolai. He was warm and sweet.

Her own lips formed a genuine smile. "Me too. Though, I do need to practice that lifting part. I still struggle to hold balance."

"We can practice it. My room has enough space-" Dale paused, clearing his throat. "I didn't mean anything with that. I really did mean practicing the routine. I-" He sighed. "I'm such an idiot. How badly did I mess up?"

A quiet chuckle burst through her lips. "You didn't. Actually, I think it's a good idea."

Relief rushed over his sunny features. "Sometimes I can act dumb when I'm around beautiful girls." Dale chuckled. "Do you wanna come over and practice then? My house isn't far from here."

"Why not." Angelique said with a smile, her cheeks flushed by the sneaky compliment.

Dale was a charmer. He never let silence settle between them. Quiet laughs and flirt was exchanged as the two left the cozy coffee shop. He was the perfect gentleman, walking closer to the driving side of the road, holding her gently by the hand, and even offering over his denim jacket when cold made her shiver.

There was no woman in this world that wouldn't want a boyfriend like him. He made her feel relaxed for the first time in very long. Perhaps she could leave those awful events behind her after all.

"Welcome to my humble home!" Dale spread out his arms as the pair entered a two story house. It was not a mansion, but certainly one of the more expensive homes in the neighborhood with ample windows and spacious rooms. "Do you want something to drink?"

"No, thank you." Angelique still stood in the doorway. Why the hell was she hesitating to enter past hallway? She had been so relaxed out on the street, and now she felt more tense than ever.

"Come on, don't just stand there. Treat this as your home. My parents are on a vacation, so it's only the two of us." Dale's voice dropped an octave. His expression was serious as he looked at her, before the smile returned. "You don't have a reason to feel nervous."

"I am not nervous." A lie. "I am just struggling to feel at home in a stranger's house."

"Ouch. We are not strangers."

"It's not really how I meant it-"

Dale chuckled. "I get it. I would be the same if I was you. Totally normal. My room is upstairs."

Ugh. Get a grip of yourself. Nothing is going to happen, why the hell you are acting so stupid!?

Angelique scolded herself, finally taking a step into the living room. Dale had mentioned his mom being an interior designer. It certainly showed. Everything was arranged with accuracy of someone caring for details and color combinations.

"It's a beautiful house." She blurt out, following him up the curved staircase. "I used to want to be a designer. Never really had the knack for it, though."

"Odd. I think you would make a wonderful designer." Dale glanced down at her over his shoulder. "You give out an impression of being good at everything."

"That's so not true." Angelique shook her head. "Opposite in fact. I am bad at so many things, it should be illegal to let me do them in first place."

"For example?"

"Parking backwards."

"Is anyone ever good at that?" He gave her a lopsided grin, closing the door behind her. His room was tidier then she had expected from a collage boy, almost as if he had cleaned it on purpose.

Dale was quick to fill the room with all too familiar beats of music, and push an arm chair to the corner to make more room. "Ready?"

Angelique nodded, dropping her bag onto his bed. Her body fell into motion, agile movements bringing her closer to the dance partner who was watching her intently. His strong arms came to rest on her thin waist, guiding her to the beat.

Swiftly, he swirled her around and lifted her above his head. Dale wasn't too muscular, but he was strong. Her weight balanced itself out, allowing his hands to adjust her into the right position. This was nothing like dancing around the pole. This wasn't just dance. It was art.

When Angelique danced, all troubles seemed to flow away. It was just them. When her feet touched the ground, she was already moving into the next step that brought their bodies close together. Dale's grip on her sides tightened more than it should, causing her to halt. Suddenly, he was no longer dancing. He was staring at her.

Angelique felt her heart flip. Without a word, he leaned closer.

"Dale-" His lips were pressed against her own in a butterfly light kiss. This was what she had been daydreaming about for ages, and now it was happening, but....

"What the hell." Angelique pushed back, creating a distance between the two.

Dale was lost for words, panting. "I-...I'm sorry. I thought you wanted this. I didn't mean to startle you."

His apology fell on deaf ears. "No." She shook her head. Anxiety surged over her in crashing waves. "I will be leaving now."

"Angel wait-"

"Don't you call me that!"

Dale had never heard her snap like this. The boy was left frozen in middle of the bedroom with the music playing in background as she rushed out. "I'm sorry! I didn't know I was doing something wrong! Please wait! I promise I won't do anything!"

She never responded. The door slammed shut behind her with a reverberating bang. Her heart was droning in her ears like war-drum. Her steps quickly carried her away from Dale's house. The girl didn't dare to slow down the jog until the building was out of sight. Only then she fell back into a normal pace, heavy breaths burning her lungs.

Angel. Why the hell did he call me Angel!?

She couldn't bear to hear that name coming from a boy she liked. He had promised to just dance, but for men, it was simply not enough.

"I'm such a fool...." She murmured, brushing back her blond hair in frustration.

Evening had already tinted the sky dark, and not many people were walking the streets. In her hurry, she hadn't been aware of her somewhat eerie surroundings, nor the footsteps that had fallen into sync with her own.

"Angel." A low, gruff voice echoed from behind her.

Chapter 10

Her entire body froze.

She knew that voice - it made her terrified to turn and confirm her suspicions. It made her chest swell with a breath she was too afraid to release. It wasn't Dale's apologetic and sunny tone. This voice demanded her to stop when all she wanted was to run as fast as her legs carried her.

"I payed off my debt." The whisper came out with a shaky exhale.

She felt him approach until his hot breath brushed against her nape. "Your father visited the club the other day."

Her eyes closed.

My god.

It wasn't a question of if. It was a question of how much.

Her mouth suddenly felt dry as a sandpaper. Her palms became damp with sweat and she was sure that they were trembling by her sides. "How....much?"

"More than one night can pay off."

Tears begun to well up in her eyes. They fogged her vision, but she refused to let them fall. Slowly, she forced herself to turn around and face him. Silver eyes caught her own, staring down at her with evil glee.

"How can I....pay it off?" She feared the question more than the tall man in front of her.

Nikolai captured her chin between his carouse fingers, tilting her head upwards as if to inspect if her features had changed. "Be mine, Angel."

How could he say those things so damn casually!? This was her life they were discussing, but he cared none for that. Angelique gulped. "How many times?"

"How many it might take."

"And what if I refuse?"

He leaned in to whisper in her ear. "You're a smart girl, you know better than to refuse."

Her jaw clenched when his teeth captured her earlobe, taunting her. The young woman wished desperately she was one of those that could keep their face indifferent in these situations. Angelique was an open book, now displaying the fear Nikolai relished in. There was something beneath his sharp gaze that oozed deep satisfaction from power he had over her.

Like a puppeteer pulling the strings of its marionette.

"I...understand." Defeat echoed in her voice. But there was also something else mixing into her tone - anger. Scalding hot and burning her inside out. For the first time she truly felt like an animal driven into a corner. "But I need time. I have to talk to my...father." She spat out the name without much emotion aside from deep hurt. 'Father' had become not much more than a label at this point.

He promised.

"I won't take you today. However, tomorrow...." Nikolai hooked his fingers through her hair. "A car will pick you up." His tone held a warning - Don't be late, don't disobey, don't dare to think of running.

His fingers untangled themselves from her hair, caressing her jawline. Coldly, he pressed a forced kiss against her closed mouth. "Until tomorrow, my Angel." Nikolai tightened his grip before releasing her altogether.

He left her standing in middle of the dark street. Angelique watched the black SUV that had been tailing her without her knowledge speed off after Nikolai had climbed inside. Finally she let the building tears to run down her cold cheeks.

On inside, she was screaming, kicking walls and ripping apart whatever was in her way, but on outside, she felt numb. Her steps dragged and tears kept coming without her permission. Why me? What did I ever do to anyone to deserve this? To be a toy for a monster....

Her father was already home when she arrived. He sat on the couch with a bottle of beer in one hand and remote in the other. "Oh! Angelique, you're home late." His voice came from the living room, oblivious to her state of well being.

"How could you?" The simple question that so numbly tumbled over her lips made him freeze and look up at his daughter who was now gazing at him with blank eyes.

"Angelique....I-"

"You promised not to gamble again."

"It was just this once! I swear I won't do it anymore! I was lucky, but they tricked me!"

"How could you do this to me!?" Her voice broke. She rarely screamed, but now she couldn't help it. All bottled emotions went spilling over the brimming glass. "Do you have any idea what I had to do to clear your debt!? And now you did it to me again! Now I can't pay it off!"

Tears filled her father's eyes. He got up from the couch, swaying slightly on his feet. Many beer bottles cluttered onto the ground. They rolled across the creaky floor with painful noise. "I'm so sorry....Please forgive me, daughter. I will find a way to pay it off myself I swear-" He slurred.

"Too late."She took a step back when he made a move to approach. Drunk and pathetic, this is how she would remember her father. A gambler with another lost job. "It's all too late..."

Angelique didn't wait for yet another excuse, rushing towards her room. She heard her dad topple onto the ground among the empty bottles, but didn't care to help him. For once she had enough. She loved him for all her life, and where did it get her!?

An old duffle bag was dragged out from her closet. It quickly filled with clothes, money she had saved up and some other necessities.

If I don't leave now, I might not have another chance.

A part of her felt it was a fools errand to attempt to escape from mafia, but she would regret it far more if she didn't try. She didn't even have a proper plan. All she knew was that she had to act now, and that distance was the only thing that mattered.

Angelique zipped up the duffle bag, tossing it over her slender shoulder. Nikolai was capable of tracking her down if she wasn't careful. Perhaps there was someone already put at her door to ensure their deal wouldn't be jeopardized.

The the window frame rattled like it always did when she pushed it open. Quick look around later, her legs were dangling from the second floor window. The roof of patio spared her a merciless fall. Her heart beat faster with every step she took. The second her flat sole boots touched the muddy ground, she took off in a sprint across the street.

Couple odd looks were given to the young woman, but most would assume she's just another teenager late for a bus. No one knew the real danger chasing after her. The train wreck her life had become. Buildings, street lights and the crowds went past her in a grey blur.

Angelique just barely caught up to an old bus that was leaving the city. Her body slumped against the uncomfortable, tattered seat, chest heaving. Ticket she had purchased was crumbled between her shaky fingers.

Safe....for now.

Her head rested against the fogged up window. With loud roar of aging engine, the bus set into motion. The bag sat in her lap, giving her an odd sense of security. Despite everything, she felt bad for leaving her dad like that. He had done awful things, but she still loved him....somehow. Would her life ever be normal again? Or would she spend it all on a run for her life?

The thought made her stomach twist in knots.

With a sigh, Angelique forced her eyes to close. She needed rest, desperately.

The chatter of people sitting behind her lulled her into a light slumber that wasn't meant to last much like her peace. What seemed to be minutes later the bus came to a harsh stop, loudly honking at a car that had suddenly appeared right in front of it.

Angelique awoke from dull pain in her forehead. The driver had hit breaks so suddenly, her head had bumped into the cold glass. With a hiss, she quickly sat up straighter, much like everyone else on the bus watching with confusion what had happened.

The front of the bus bust open and two men clad in black got inside.

Hell no....Please, no!

Chapter 11

Color drained from her face. First man turned to talk to the driver and the other scanned the crowd of passengers. She quickly recognized who this particular guy was. His cold, unwavering stare fell onto her, shattering any hopes of safe escape.

Dog made his way through the rows of seats, pinning her with a malicious leer. Angelique pressed herself deeper into the seat, wishing it could absorb her. If a black hole appeared beneath her feet, she would happily let it swallow her up.

Her wide blue eyes fell to the ground - like that would do a damn. She didn't dare to look up when he came stand besides her. The cold gaze drilled holes in her skull.

"Come with me." Dog said dully. The firm tone spoke louder then words - answer no was not an option.

When Angelique didn't move, he leaned in closer. "Don't cause a fuss. Come with me or I will shoot everyone on this bus, and drag you out of here."

She saw the metal of his gun gleam where it was strapped to his belt. Without a word, she stood up and followed Dog to the front of the bus.The driver looked terrified enough to pee his pants. Whatever the other man had said, it had left the poor man ghostly white. Angelique could only manage a glance his way, before her upper arm was seized, and she was dragged out from the bus.

"Get inside." Dog ordered, jutting his chin towards a familiar black SUV. "And don't think of anything stupid." He threatened, giving her upper arm a warning squeeze.

Nervously, Angelique shambled into the backseat, door slamming and locking seconds later.

"I thought you were a smart girl." An accent rich voice instantly caught her attention. Nikolai sat besides her, his facial expression one of stone. "Not that I wasn't expecting that. Did you really think you could escape me?" He didn't look at her. His jaw remained taunt, muscles in his cheeks moving with the clenching and unclenching teeth.

Angelique had pressed herself firmly against the locked car door, putting as much distance between her and the imposing man as possible.

"You left me no other choice...." Shockingly she managed to keep her voice steady. And that gave her an unexpected boost of stupid bravery. "You think you can just waltz back into my life. We had a deal, and I did my part...." Her stomach clenched at the bitter sweet memory. "I don't want to be involved in my father's debts anymore-"

"You rather see him dead?"

The question chilled to the bone. Answer was simple - no. He wasn't the best man or father, but he still had a place in her heart.

Nikolai turned to look at her. Having his eyes on her was like by accident taking the ice bucket challenge. It got her breath to halt and goosebumps to spread along her fore-arms. "It's a simple question, Angel." He stared at her with a clear demand.

How the hell could she answer to something like that with-out having her wings clipped!?

Who am I trying to fool...my wings were clipped long ago.

"No."

In a heartbeat Nikolai reached over, capturing her chin in his hand. "You traded your freedom for his life long ago." His thumb flicked across her bottom lip. "I've been too soft on you. I need to punish you for trying to break our deal."

The car skid to a sudden halt. Smell of burning rubber from screeching tires attacked on her delicate senses. Adrenaline rushed through her veins, and her eyes widened in horror. "Please don't do that." Her meek pleading was ignored.

Nikolai released her jaw, getting out from the SUV without second glance at the trembling woman. Angelique barely held her balance when her side of the door flew open. Dog yanked her from the car seat. She was jolted forwards by a firm hand wrapped around her upper arm.

Her gut flipped at the sight of gloom warehouse. Its con-crete walls, rusted iron constructions and shattered win-dows made it look like a movie set for a horror film. No one would hear her screams coming from within. No one would rush to her aid.

"Let go." Angelique felt the panic surge up in rapid waves. The blond hair around her face had become tousled from the struggling. Her feet dragged across the cement, and no matter how many times she dug her heels into the ground, she was harshly pushed to move forwards.

Nikolai walked calmly ahead of her. He heard her protests but no reaction followed, like he had a far better response in mind.

The door to the warehouse opened from inside, revealing more of his armed goons. Her fight against Dog's vice grip become frantic. "Please, let me go-" She was pushed inside the shadowy, dust layered building. Smell of mold and blood hit her instantly. The moist air was heavy with unpleasant smells. A lonely bulb illuminated the ample space, leaving most of it enveloped in pitch black darkness.

Underneath the poor light stood three men, but that wasn't what got her heart to stop pounding. Between the dark silhouettes was a girl, forced to her knees and shaking. Her form was naked, aside from underwear, and littered by countless bruises.

Dried blood and tears stuck to her sunken cheeks. Her eyes were red and swollen, one of them sporting a huge, near black shiner. Her lip was bust open, leaking ruby red. If it wasn't for the fact that she had known this woman for the longest time, she might've not recognized her beaten form.

"Amanda...." Angelique choked out.

"You see, my Angel," Nikolai spoke coldly, pulling out a metallic chair. "You forced my hand, and now I have to teach you a lesson." He sat down, lightening a cigarette. His gaze held a storm while the rest of his face appeared emotionless. "Rape her." The words rung authority. Cold and brutal.

Angelique's eyes widened in utter horror. "No! Don't do it! Please!" Dog grabbed both of her arms, forcing her smaller frame against his own.

The three men grabbed ahold of Amanda. Her scrams filled the warehouse as she was forced to the damp ground. Her friend's cries sent chilling fear down her spine. One of the three men held down Amanda's arms, the other grasped her legs, spreading them apart for the third man to tower over her particularly naked form.

"Please, Nikolai! Make it stop!" Angelique begged. "It's my fault, don't punish her for my choices! I beg you!"

Nikolai remained stone-faced. He wasn't even slightly disturbed by what was happening. His ruthless silver eyes gazed at the panicking Angelique, but he didn't order his men to stop.

It was like world had come to a stand still. She saw the cigarette smoke swirl and disappear, she heard distant screams of her friend, and shuffling of clothes. And then, everything happened all at once. Like some unknown force had taken over her, Angelique stomped on Dog's foot with all her might. With a low growl, he released her from his fierce hold. She set into motion before he could grab her again.

Her knees bent to her will, forcing her down on the ground in front of Nikolai. Angelique crumbled in front of him, her fingers digging into the fabric of his shirt, and desperate tear filled eyes gazed up at his own. "Please..." She begged again. "I will never disobey you again. I am yours, but please, make it stop."

For a good moment he stared down at her before his hand raised, and all motion behind them stopped. The three men took a step back from Amanda, leaving her shaking onto the ground. Nikolai's eyes never left Angelique's tear ridden face. Slowly, he lowered his arm, caressing her cheek with unforeseen gentleness. Something in his eyes had changed - dare she say, softened.

"I like seeing you on your knees, Angel." His deep voice leaked satisfaction, his hand trailing to grab her hair instead. With a sharp tug, he had her neck bending backwards all the way. "I hope you have realized that you can't escape me." His teeth bared into a cruel smile. "You're mine, do you understand?" He tugged on her hair painfully.

Angelique shook her head. "I...I understand. P-please....d on't hurt her....She is innocent." She sobbed.

Nikolai took a long look at her face, his fingers untangling themselves from her golden locks before they had ripped a hole in her scalp. "Don't ever challenge me like this again. I won't be forgiving next time." He suddenly stood up, towering over her in full length. "Attend to your friend, we are leaving in ten."

Chapter 12

The small, cramped bedroom withheld an eerie silence. Only sound was the old window rattling from the harsh wind outside. Angelique sat on the side of an old mattress, staring at an empty wall as if it held any meaning. "It's all my fault." She blurt out. "If I hadn't run, none of this would've happened to you."

Silence.

The blonde took a deep, shaky breath, turning her eyes downward to the lump underneath a thick duvet. Messy brunette hair stuck out from the covers that raised and fell with unsteady sobs. "I don't expect you to forgive me."

Silence.

"Please, say something.....anything."

"It's not your fault." A raspy whisper came from underneath the covers. "I don't blame you. It's that monster...." Amanda chocked out another sob.

"I can't begin to explain how this happened."

"We need to call the police." The blanket flew off, revealing a disheveled person. Her eye was swollen shut and her lip had taken a purplish shade."Pass me the phone, we have to do it quick-"

"No." Angelique shook her head, grasping her friend's fragile arms. "I wouldn't be surprised if they have corrupted the police. We can't risk it." She took a side glance at the window. She could see the black SUV parked down the street, waiting. Nikolai had allowed her to take Amanda to her house. Fifteen minutes from the twenty allowed had already passed.

"What are you saying then?" Amanda pulled her hands to herself. "They almost raped me! They kidnapped me! And they are doing all these awful things to you! And you don't want to call the police!?" Her voice trembled with outrage.

"Listen, if we call the police, there's a chance of much worse things happening. I will figure something out, I promise....I have to go now." Angelique stood up. "Promise me you won't do anything. I don't want to see you dead."

Amanda tensed, staring up at her friend. "Fine. But this conversation isn't over. We can't let this happen." Her beaten face was pulled into a deep scowl. Thousands of thoughts rushed through her head all at once, before she seemed to settle down and finally agree with her friend. Her body was still quivering, and she looked like she was a hair away from breaking down again.

"I have to go." Angelique cast her eyes downwards. "I will call first chance I have."

"Promise?"

"I promise."

"Don't let them do anything to you-"

Angelique closed the door gently. That was something she couldn't promise. Sucking in a deep breath, she left Amanda's apartment. Wind had picked up, whipping at her pale cheeks and tossing about her blond hair. It was a short walk from the front door to her unavoidable fate.

Dog stood leaning against the front of the car, his eyes nailed on the woman the second she had left her friend's place. Nikolai had allowed them twenty minutes of solitude, but never had left. Their business wasn't done.

"I can open my own doors." Angelique murmured when Dog pointed her to the backseat. Little to no ones surprise she didn't get much response.

Leather hugged around her figure as she took a seat in otherwise rather comfortable car. She much rather choose to think about the SUV than the imposing man sitting besides her. His eyes were burning holes in her flesh. He stared with intensity of a wolf eyeing up its dinner.

"Are you scared of me, Angel?" His voice rumbled the second the car set into motion.

"Are you seriously asking me that?"

"Answer." He demanded.

Angelique turned her head to face him. "Yes. I have every right to be."

Nikolai ran a hand through his neatly groomed walnut color hair, slicking them back with easy motion. Not a single hair was out of place. Monster he was, but he certainly didn't look like one. The man took great care of his outer appearance. "It was for your own sake." He said matter-of-factly.

"How so?" She scowled, feeling the daring protest return ten fold, only smoldered by her own mind that told her to do the vise thing, and remain silent. But the fire in her eyes had spoken before her lips did, and it did not fly by him unnoticed.

"You had to understand what it means to defy me." Nikolai reached out to touch her hair. The locks of gold had charmed him the first time he had laid eyes on them. Man of such brutality...it was almost miracle that he was capable of something that didn't inflict pain.

Angelique pressed herself further against the locked door, but couldn't escape his caress. "Your life won't be the same anymore," He continued. "It's for the best if you learn fast to accept it." His fingers released the tips of her hair, falling back to rest on his lap.

Uncomfortable silence settled among them. She almost preferred it to talking to him. Angelique made sure her gaze only remained on the rushing scenery outside the tinted window. From time to time she felt his eyes on her, but didn't react to it.

An hour or so later, the car parked in front of somewhat familiar gate. White mansion lingered in distance, sending a chill to crawl down her spine.

"From now on, you're going to live here." Nikolai's voice boomed, providing her with an answer she had feared to hear.

Servants had lined up by the large oak door, bowing their heads when they got out from the car as if Nikolai was a royalty. An uneasy feeling settled in her gut. Both intimidating men flanking either side of her, Angelique was lead inside the luxurious building. It oozed riches and power gained with hands drenched in blood.

"Take her to her room." Nikolai spoke to no one in particular.

A timid maid stepped forwards, giving Angelique a look of pity. "Follow me, Miss." She instructed quietly.

"Get some rest, Angel." Nikolai whispered in her ear, his hand falling on the small of her back to give her a nudge forwards. "I will see you later."

She felt his eyes linger on her back. Angelique followed the maid upstairs to a large bedroom. Like everything else in the house it was decorated for those of noble blood. A rich red canopy hanged from carved wooden frames around the bed, matching the color of thick velvety curtains.

Even the golden threads in decorative pillows scattered atop the billowy mattress looked like they were from real gold. For someone used to sleeping on a bunk bed with spirals sticking out where it had been the most slept in, this seemed like a dream. Or a well presented nightmare.

Like a glorified prisoner put in a golden cage....

"I hope, it suits your liking, miss." The maid spoke once Angelique had taken a step inside the room.

Her answer didn't come right away. "Are you a captor as well?"

The question seemed to throw the poor maid off guard. "What do you mean by that, miss?"

"Were you forced here as well?"

"No, miss. I've worked for Ivanov family since young age. I am treated well, like everyone else who remains loyal." The maid explained, a tad hesitant. "My name is Irina. I am trusted to assist you, if you ever need anything. Please call for me if there ever is a need." She gave a short bow before hurriedly excusing herself.

Angelique was left completely alone with her thoughts and sumptuousness she never asked for.

Idly, she wondered if this would be her prison for the remains of her life. Will she ever be set free from him? Who else he was willing to hurt to make her stay?

Her head fell into her hands. She wanted to weep like a lost child, but no tears came out. Finally, she had cried to her limit.

Angelique sunk onto the ground, curling up against the nearest wall with a single question lingering in her head.

What the hell is that monster going to do to me next?

Chapter 13

"**M**iss!" A distressed voice echoed through the darkness.

"Miss! Please wake up!"

Angelique felt her shoulders being shaken, dragging her out from deep slumber she had so naively hoped to never awake from. Slowly, her heavy lashed peeled open. Fist thing she saw was a worried expression of Irina. The maid was leaning over her where she had passed out yesterday, still slumped against the wall.

"Thank God," Irina sighed when she saw her eyes finally open. "Are you alright, miss? Do you want me to call a doctor?"

"No." She croaked. Her vocal cords were dry as sandpaper. "Don't call anyone." It hadn't been a nightmare after all. The gilded cage was just as real as the invisible shackles on her wrists and heavy weights on her shoulders.

"Are you sure? You look pale." Irina pressed.

"I said I'm fine." She didn't mean to snap. Irina was not to blame for what had happened. "I'm sorry. I didn't meant to-"

"It's quite alright, miss." The dark haired woman gave her a wry smile. "I will draw you a bath."

Angelique wanted to protest, but no words came out. Her eyes stopped at a box Irina was holding. As if to read her thoughts, the woman explained, "It's a dress. Mr. Ivanov wants you to wear it when you eat dinner tonight."

"Dinner...with him?"

"Of course. He has requested your presents." Irina handed her the box before shuffling off to the bathroom. Sound of running water drummed against her ears. She felt her stomach coil at the thought of seeing that man again. Peering into the box, she found a beautiful white dress and set of matching color lingerie. Her fingers trembled and the lump in her throat made it impossible to breath.

"You were asleep for a long time. I was beginning to worry." Irina's voice cut through her troubled thoughts. Shortly after, the maid emerged from the lavish bathroom, thin smile on her lips. "Your bath will be ready soon. I shall leave you to it, but please do call if you need anything." Her gaze lingered, awaiting a response that never came.

After the black haired woman had left, eerie silence settled in the room. Angelique drew in a deep breath.

Be brave.

The warm water hardly soothed the wreck that had become of her nerves. She wished more than ever that minutes would turn into hours, anything to keep her from coming face to face with that monster. Angelique sat inside the bath until the water had become cold and her fingers had wrinkled.

A whole hour later, she was dressed and ready. Irina had returned to help her with her hair and make up. Her breaths were shallow and her fingers clung to the soft material of her dress as the maid lead her down the waving hallways to the dining room.

Nikolai was already waiting when she entered. He sat like a king at the end of the table, his unyielding gaze stopping her in her tracks. His tattooed arms were set on full display with his black shirt rolled up. Heat spread through her like wildfire when he sized her up from head to toe.

A satisfied hum rumbled through his chest. "You look lovely." His voice was hoarse and his expression one of stone. She couldn't read what he was thinking, but she saw the heat dancing beneath those sharp grey eyes.

"Sit." He ordered.

Angelique hesitated before settling into a chair across from him. Nikolai looked greatly dissatisfied by this, but didn't say a word. His stare never wavered, she felt it burning her skin even when she refused to meet it. Her eyes were cast down towards empty plate in front of her.

"You think I'm a monster, don't you?" His voice rumbled, forcing her to look back up. Nikolai stroked his chin, lips pulled in thin line.

Be brave.

"You have proven yourself to be a monster." Angelique spoke, her soft, feminine voice a stark contrast to his rough tone.

Nikolai regarded her in silence for a moment longer. "You really don't remember me, huh?"

This made her frown deeply. "Remember you?" Before the night in club she had never met him.

He didn't respond to that. The man sunk back into the chair, thick eyebrows knit together. "Does the room suit your taste, Angel?" He changed the topic, leaving her deeply confused.

"I like it as much as I would like a prison cell."

"You won't lack anything here. You belong to me now, and I will ensure you have everything you could ever want. You just have to tell me."

"I want my freedom."

The look in his eyes sharpened. "Everything besides that."

"Then I need nothing from you." Silence settled between them, broken by sound of servants entering with platters of food. Nikolai didn't spare them a single glance. He didn't look away from her as if she would poof in the thin air if he did.

Delicious smell made her stomach growl in demand. She hadn't realized how hungry she was until now. Hungry enough to disregard his unwavering gaze. They ate in silence for a while until a thought crossed her mind.

"There is one thing I want from you." Angelique said halfway through the meal. Nikolai didn't say anything, but she knew he was listening. She felt his eyes on her. "There's a dance competition coming up. I have the lead role. I want to....attend it." Dance was her life. She had put in her sweat and blood to prepare for it. Fate might've twisted her life beyond recognition, but there was nothing she wished more than to participate.

Nikolai looked like he was pondering the idea. "No." The single sharp word cut through like a knife.

"Dancing is all I have left. Please." She looked into his steely silver eyes.

"I like it when you beg." The cruel words sparked hope, that was quick to turn into dread. "I will allow it if you earn it."

Suddenly the food was crawling its way back up her throat. "How?" The question sent waves of terror through her. What other monstrous thing did he have in store for her?

"With your body."

Chapter 14

The room was enveloped in darkness. Curtains pulled close, she could only see slivers of moonlight slipping through the gaps. One of those dim beams fell over the walnut color locks of Nikolai's hair. It gave his face a sharp edge and made his grey eyes shine predatory silver. His jaw was clenched, looking sharp enough to cut through skin.

Slowly, he lifted a dark looking drink to his lips, his Adams apple bobbing with the massive gulp. Still, his eyes didn't leave her trembling form.

You will earn what you want with your body. That's what he had said.

"Undress." The single-word order shook the air around them, spoken in tone so low and gravelly she felt her bones quiver.

The dress had become crumpled where she had been clenching it the entire way to his bedroom. It was far more extensive than her own. Darkness forbid her to see many details, but she could clearly make out the outlines of tall bookshelves. Nikolai sat perched in an armchair set in front of them, whiskey swirling in the glass he held.

Finally her cramping fingers released the dress. The thin straps fell from her slender shoulders and soon the dress was laying in a heap at her feet. Angelique exhaled shakily, reaching behind her to undo the hook of her bra.

"Leave that on." Nikolai took another sip from his drink, his gaze lingering. Deep satisfaction ran through him at the sigh of her in the lingerie he had bought for her. "Kneel." His eyes followed hungrily as she sunk onto her knees between his legs.

Her trembling fingers dragged down the zipper of his trousers and undid the belt. He was already hard, the thick shaft pressing against the fabric of his underwear.

"Have you done this before?" His hand combed through her hair, the silky locks twisting and twirling around his long fingers. The movement was so gentle it could be mistaken by care. She knew better than that. He was ruthless. A man of sheer control and hunger for power. Someone like him wasn't capable of genuine gentleness or love.

"No. I sold my virginity to you." Angelique swallowed, pushing back all the emotions that came surging over her in waves.

"You could've done this without losing your virginity." He said. "Such an innocent little Angel..." His voice said he wanted to add something to that, but no words followed. Instead his grip on her hair tightened, bringing her lips closer to his erection. "Bite me and you will regret it."

Don't tempt me.

If she had been braver, perhaps she would've done just that. But Nikolai's wrath wasn't something she was willing to challenge after what he had done to Amanda. The thick tip pushed past her lips, intruding into her mouth. Angelique flinched with the swift thrust of his hips, her jaw aching. His grip on her golden hair tightened, his hand guiding her head into the movement.

A low growl rumbled through his chest, his head lulling back in pleasure. She was not experienced with this and yet he looked like he was close to heaven. He didn't give her any breaks, his shaft pushing deeper into her mouth with every movement. Any faster and her jaw would dislocate. Nikolai was rough, and the closer to climax he was, the more she felt she wouldn't survive this experience.

"Teeth." He warned when her teeth brushed against his shaft. Her lips hurt and her throat was on fire. Tears begun to fill her eyes when his hips joined, thrusting himself deeper into her mouth. The rugged breaths turned into low groans and then she felt him stiffen inside her. Warm liquid trailed down her throat without her consent.

When he pulled out of her mouth, Angelique gasped for air. She crumbled at his feet, breathing unsteadily.

"You did good." Nikolai praised, all the wild emotions he had expressed when she pleased him slipping behind a facade. He had come undone underneath her touch, and just as easily he was once more the cruel leader of mafia. Only his somewhat heavy breathing suggested that anything had happened in the first place. "You have earned your dance competition." He said simply, zipping back up his pants and pouring himself another glass of whiskey.

That's it? He doesn't want to continue?

Confusion seeped onto her features. A part of her was relieved he didn't request anything else, but then there was this other feeling she couldn't quite pinpoint. He had her once and now he didn't want her anymore? Would he get rid of her once he grows bored?

Sensing her eyes on him, Nikolai glanced down at her. "Is there anything else you want, Angel?"

"No." The young woman hurriedly averted her gaze.

"You may leave then."

He was tossing her out like a used toy. Angelique felt her blood boil. He was treating her like she wasn't even there anymore. Smart thing would be to take the chance to leave, but something made her linger. "Can I ask you a question?"

His cold eyes settled back onto her. "Hm?"

"What you said before....What did you mean when you said that I don't remember you?"

He stared at her for a long moment. "You will have to do far more than a blowjob to earn that answer." Nikolai stood up, setting the half full glass aside. "I want you to find out the answer to that yourself, Angel." He towered over her, serious look on his face. "Once you do....I will set you free."

Her eyes widened at that.

He's going to set me free?

Nikolai caressed her cheek with the back of his hand. There was something akin to longing in his gaze. The single emotion made her shudder. His grey eyes held a deep look in them, one that called out to her soul and made her heart beat faster in her chest.

The moment had lasted only for a fleeting second. He dropped his hand and the coldness was back.

"Now go, before I change my mind."

Chapter 15

Days rolled by in a blur and eventually marked a week since she first arrived at Ivanov mansion. Time had an odd flow there. It dragged during the lonely days and flew by in a flash when Nikolai and her had dinner. It had become a tradition of sorts. When he wasn't off running the club, he made sure that they had meals together. Sometimes they barely exchanged a word, but sometimes they talked for hours like two normal people, like she wasn't his prisoner and he wasn't her cruel captor.

Angelique had learned things about him she had never expected to know. Nikolai hated pickles and always kept a gun under his pillow. Somewhere along the lines she had slipped a story or two about her own life. He always listened intently, even if he never commented on any of them. It was an odd exchange.

While he never let the mask fall, she was beginning to see signs of human nature. He got irritated when she asked one too many questions and he was pleased when she wore white and let her blond hair loose.

He had even allowed her to attend school again, but only if Dog was following her. Everyone had freak out at the sight of her new bodyguard at first. Honestly, she couldn't blame them. That man always wore a scowl as part of his all-black attire and never spoke a word unless it was absolutely necessary.

The day of the competition had arrived before she had the time to blink. People were bustling around the backstage, rushing about and arranging the props. Groups of dancers were gathering around, chatting among themselves and warming up.

To think that after she had stripped naked in front of a horny crowd, she would feel a tad less nervous now. Hell no. Her nerves were wrecking havoc inside her. Angelique shifted her weight from one leg to another, practicing the silly, yet oddly helpful breathing expertise she had picked up from the internet.

"Calm down. We're going to nail it." Dale spoke up besides her, offering a small, comforting smile. It had been a while since they last talked. Since she took off running things had been awkward between them. He had apologized and they had set thighs straight. It was fairly obvious when things weren't quite as they should be between the two lead dancers. Both of them were grown ups and professionals. Mulling over what had happened would ruin their act.

"Where's your scary bodyguard?"

"Somewhere around here I think." Angelique let a soft chuckle slip past her lips. Dog had wandered off somewhere, and she finally felt that she could breathe.

"That dude is scary. Why is he here anyway?" Dale questioned, mix of concern and curiosity playing through his sunny tone.

"Dad hired him. I got mugged and he overreacted." A lie. She had learned to tell this story swiftly. What else could she possibly say?

I got myself in shit with Russian mob and now their boss or whatever is keeping me on leash?

Bah. She could only imagine what face Dale would make at that.

"That's awful. I hope you're okay." Gently, he took ahold of her hand, giving it a reassuring squeeze. His hand was so warm, his skin soft like he hadn't worked a day in his life. Dale's touch was nothing like Nikolai's. His hands were callous and his gentlest touch could be considered rough. It never failed to make her shiver.

Speakers came to life, announcing the next group to come up on the stage. Dale squeezed her hand tighter. "Here goes nothing." He mumbled.

Angelique breathed out a nervous sight, letting her partner lead her up on the stage. The white lights were near blinding. Loud applause filled the hall. The gathering crowd was larger than she had anticipated. Jury set at the front, already taking notes when the dancers flowed into their spots.

Angelique leaned over Dale's arm, arching her back and pointing her toes. Her eyes dropped close and with the first beat of music, she swirled into motion. All stress seemed to dissipate. She knew the routine by heart, allowed her body to move and her mind be free.

Everything went smoothly until....

She glanced at the crowd. There, leaning against the wall, shrouded by shadows was a man with piercing grey eyes; watching. Her breath hitched and her body stammered. Just like the first time she danced in the club, her movements stalled and her heart pounded.

He's here.

The thought bounced back and forth in her head. Her chest suddenly felt tight, illusion of freedom shattering like brittle glass.

It was already too late to fix the slip up. Dale rushed to her aid, pulling her into the next swirl. Her body obeyed, but her head was no longer in the dance. When their act came to an end, and wave of applause sounded through the hall, she didn't enjoyed the attention.

Something in her had twisted. When she looked back at the place where he was standing, Nikolai was gone as if he wasn't there in the first place. Was her mind playing tricks on her?

"What happened?" Dale questioned the second they got off the stage. "You froze."

"I-" She swallowed. "I don't know. I'm sorry."

"You're so pale. You didn't see a ghost did you?" He teased, attempting to lighten the mood. "Come here, let's get you some water." Before she could protest, he took her by the hand and lead her into an empty changing room. "This was

your first big performance. Things like that happen. Seriously, are you okay? You look spooked."

Angelique took the glass of water he offered. "I'm fine. I
just...thought I saw someone. I should go apologize to others.
We might've lost because of me."

"Wait," Dale once again took ahold of her hand. "There's
something I want to tell you..." He trailed off. "I like you. A
lot."

Oh, no, no, no.

"Dale-"

"Hear me out, please." The grip of her hand tightened. "I
have had feelings for you since I first saw you. You are a
gorgeous girl, and you're sweet and kind. I could go on and
on. I want you to be my girlfriend." He tugged her closer to
his body, his other arm wrapping around her waist. "I haven't
felt this way about anyone else. Please....go out with me."

This was the moment she had dreamed about since she
first met the collage sweetheart. Things would be so easy if
she was his girlfriend. They would make a good couple. It had
felt so right before, and she had imagined it more than once;
them walking down the street holding hands and eating ice
cream.

But now, when he was looking down at her with hopeful
eyes it felt....wrong.

His grip tightened on her waist, his face drawing nearer.
"Please....Angelique..."

"I'm sorry-"

BANG!

Both of them flinched when the door to changing room slammed open. The noise of the handle smashing against the wall reverberate through the air.

Her heart fell to her gut when her gaze flashed with stormy grays.

"Nikolai...."

His teeth were grit, muscles in his jaw taunt. His eyes swirled with something she hadn't seen in them before. Raw, bloody anger.

Chapter 16

"You betrayed me."

She knew that tone. And she knew that look as well. His eyes glistened with cruelty. Cold. Unforgiving. When he last looked at her like this, she was begging for him to spare Amanda.

"Angel, angel." He shook his head. "I am disappointed. Was I naive to think that you have learned your lesson?" He spoke, retrieving two leather gloves from his black coat. He tugged them on, moving his long fingers as if to check the fit.

Her breath clogged up her throat. Dog and two other men entered the changing room. The click of lock turning made the blood freeze in her bones.

"Angelique, what's going on? Do you know them?" The brash confidence had been wiped from Dale's voice. His face was pale as a sheet, and the grip on her waist loosened as his hand trembled.

"Nikolai..I can explain. Don't hurt him. Please." She stepped back from her dance partner, struggling to keep her voice steady. "He didn't do anything. I swear-" Angelique cut herself off when one of the men suddenly kicked Dale hard enough to send him toppling onto the floor.

"No!"

Another kick.

"Stop!"

A deafening crunch followed a pained moan - the awful sound of bones breaking.

"I said stop!" Angelique lunged for one of the men. She wanted to claw out their eyes. These men hurt innocent people and for what!? To please a monster. To save their asses from his wrath. Cowards. Every fucking one of them.

Two strong arms wrapped around her waist, familiar scent filling her nose. Nikolai held her from behind, his shredded chest pressing against her back. "Shhh. You just have to watch." He whispered lowly. With ease he held her from interrupting the merciless beating. She felt him smile against her skin as his lips trailed up the side of her neck. "Enjoy the show, Angel. You brought it upon yourself."

Dale had curled up in a ball on the ground, wailing. His arms covered his head in a weak attempt to protect himself. He had begged them to stop, but now all he could manage were odd gurgling noises. Blood splattered on the ground.

Violent sobs shook her body. She kicked and screamed, but Nikolai's grip on her never eased. He held her like a vice, savoring her torment.

"You're mine, Angel. Mine alone." He reminded, the gloved hands pressing harder against her flesh.

Soon all noises died down. She had slumped against his chest, limp. Her bloodshot eyes stared down at the still figure laying in its own blood. Dale's sunny features were now far beyond recognition. Swollen and bloody. His chest no longer raised to inhale. His blue eyes didn't have the spark of life in them. They were empty and distant.

He was dead.

Dog prodded his body with the side of his boot as if the boy was nothing but trash at his feet.

"Get rid of the body." Nikolai ordered. His arms released her, allowing her to sink onto her knees.

Angelique heard him say something, but couldn't make out the words. She stared at the mutilated corpse. No crying. No begging. Something inside her had snapped. Odd emptiness took place in her soul. She didn't even flinch when Nikolai knelt down besides her. His large hand cupped her shoulder, but even then she didn't turn to look at him.

He's going to destroy everything...Kill everyone. I can't escape him.

Suddenly her head was spinning. She felt sick. Really sick.

Her hands fell flat on the tiled floor where blood was pooling around her. She couldn't breath either. Like air itself had been stolen. Nikolai's grip on her shoulder tightened and she heard him speak again, but nothing beyond the sound of his voice mattered. Men around her shuffled, one taking Dale's body by the arms to drag it away. Path of deep red stayed imprinted on the ground.

The nausea got worse. Like all strength had been sucked from her bones, she collapsed into the blood. Then there was sound of yelling. Nikolai flipped her on her back.

Those deep grey eyes stared down at her with emotion she couldn't understand. A man like him didn't feel empathy or sorrow. His lips moved but this time she couldn't hear his voice either. Her eyes had grown heavy. Black swallowed her vision and she welcomed the sensation like an old friend.

Emptiness and peace. Perhaps she could escape him after all....

Everything around them was damp and smelled like mold. It was cold. She stared down at the boy laying in her lap, gently waving her fingers through his light brown hair. They were silk soft. He wasn't older then fifteen, but his features were hardened like ones of a man. His eyes were closed, long lashes brushing against his cheeks.

"You're safe." Angelique whispered, her voice of high pitch. Her hands were small and slightly round. She was just a child too. Both of them were, even if he was older. And both of them were lost.

"You're safe." She repeated.

The boy grimaced like he was in pain, exhaling a pained breath. And then his eyes opened....

"Ah!" A sharp gasp escaped her lips. Angelique awoke with a start, her entire body coming to life all at once. Familiar ceiling stared back at her. More than one night she had spend gazing up at them in darkness, pondering what life had in stash for her.

Steadying her breath, she slowly sat up. A part of her had hoped not to wake up, but there she was, in her golden cage. An IV drip was attached to her arm, transparent liquid slowly flowing into her veins. She couldn't remember how she got there, but she did remember the rest. The blood. The cries of agony when Dale was beaten to death. And the snap.

She couldn't be sure if it had been the snapping of his bones shattering or something inside her own body. Physically nothing hurt, but the hole ripped through her chest had filled itself with bitter pain.

droplets of blood dripped onto the white sheets. She pulled the needle from her arm. Her legs were shaky, just barely capable of holding her weight when she stood. The room was near pitch black, much like her heart. It felt blackened by something fierce and demanding. An unknown force was driving her to walk, a single thought running ramp in her head.

I can't escape him. No. I have to escape him. I have to.....I have to...

She opened a drawer of her nightstand. A kitchen knife gleamed in darkness. A couple of days ago she had snatched it from Irina's cart. It was just for safety, but now the purpose had changed entirely.

Her slender fingers stroked across the cold, sharp edge.

I have to....

Even in her head she feared those words.

She inhaled shakily. Her eyes dropped close and her grip on the knife tightened. As if her legs had mind of their own, she walked out from her room towards Nikolai's bedroom.

She had only been there once or twice. He was a very private man, never letting her stay for longer than he needed her for.

Nikolai never touched her since she sold her virginity to him. He never forced himself on her like she had expected him to. She saw the desire in his eyes, felt how much he resisted taking out his primal need on her. But still he hadn't....

He was strange. A strange monster.

Perhaps after this she wouldn't be any better.

Her steps halted in front of his door. Light seeped through the cracks. He wasn't sleeping.

Angelique tested the weight of the knife in her hand.

I have to.....

She gulped.

I have to....

Her heart beat faster in her chest as she pushed the door open.

I have to kill him.

Chapter 17

Cracking fire from the fireplace cast an orange glow across the room. There he was, sitting in an armchair with glass of whiskey dangling from his long fingers. He held it so loosely it could drop and spill any moment. His back was facing her. She could only see the shack of his thick hair and his arm.

The lush carpet muffled her footsteps. Angelique sneaked across the large bedroom, her firm resolve now wavering with heaviness of the crime she was about to commit. He hadn't hesitated when he ordered Dale killed. He didn't blink when Amanda was beaten and almost raped. Violence came as easy for him as breathing, and there she was, shaken to the core from thought of his blood on her hands alone.

Desire to barf and bolt increased with each uncertain step. But she couldn't. Not after everything he had done to her... .to all those innocent people.

Knife held in white-knuckled grip, she rounded the armchair. The least she could do was give him the courtesy of knowing who killed him. Her eyes landed on him.

Nikolai's chest rose and fell with shallow breaths. His eyes were closed and his features far softer.

He's asleep. She noted.

I'm about to kill a sleeping man.

The idea didn't sit right with her. This could be her only chance, yet she hesitated to bring the knife to his throat.

Suck it up.

Her hand didn't move.

Do it! A dark voice within her urged.

Hesitantly, she brought the knife to the side of his neck. Her eyes closed. Angelique couldn't do this while seeing his peaceful expression. He looked too human. It was harder to remember the terrible things he did.

Dale's face flashed in her memory, his warm smile and then the blood. How many more lives would he ruin if she didn't do this? What her own life would become if she did?

"What are you planning on doing with that, Angel?" Deep, calm voice echoed.

Her eyes snapped open. Nikolai was gazing up at her coldly. His features had once again hardened. The peaceful expression he wore when sleeping was wiped, replaced by sternness of a mob boss.

Angelique froze, the edge of the knife inches from his throat. Inches from her freedom. She had the upper hand, and yet, with his eyes piercing through her, she couldn't finish what she came to do.

"You killed my friend." She stated. "You abused Amanda...." Her voice trembled.

"I know." For a man with a knife to his throat, he spoke very calmly, like he knew she wouldn't carry out the deed.

This irked her. A lot. "You're a fucking monster."

"I know."

She grit her teeth. "Why? Why did you do this to me?"

He remained silent for a moment, his steady gaze trailing down her features, as if he was trying to carve every subtle curve into his memory. "I'm a selfish man, Angel."

"That's it? That's the best answer you can give me after killing my friend!?" She roared. The edge of the knife drew blood. He didn't even flinch when a thin trickle ran down to the collar of his shirt. "I will kill you." She really wanted to, but her hand still refused to move.

Damnit!

"Is that so?" Hint of...amusement....played through his features. One thick eyebrow arched upwards, taunting her. "I think not, Angel." Large hand encircled her wrist. He didn't move the knife from his throat, but the grip of her wrist had secured her arm so that she wouldn't be able to slice into his skin further. "If you wanted to kill me, I would be dead already."

She hated how true those words were.

"I hate you." Tears begun to blur her vision. She refused to let them spill. "I hate you so much."

"I know." With a sharp tug, he pulled her into his lap. She straddled his long legs, felt the warmth radiating from his muscular body. "I am supposed to be hated." Nikolai whispered against her lips. "You're supposed to hate me."

His grip on her wrist tightened, forcing her to drop the knife. It cluttered onto the ground with a dull noise. "I want to have you all for myself. When that kid touched you, I couldn't let him live. You're mine. " His nose brushed against the side of her face. He inhaled her scent. "And you keep forgetting that. Our promise."

Her eyes widened. Our promise. That sparked something long forgotten. She felt a sharp tug in her chest, but she couldn't remember.

"What promise?" She whispered.

He didn't respond. Instead his arms wrapped around her waist, lifting her further into his lap. "You're mine." He repeated. "My pure little Angel." His lips brushed against her cheek. It sent a rogue shiver down her spine. How wrong it felt to feel this way towards someone she just wanted to kill. His touch was supposed to be revolting, but it was not. He was gentle, murmuring sweet nothings in her ear.

"You can't escape me."

Those words echoed through her head over and over again. "I will make sure you have no one to run off to but me." He spoke, his thumb circling her wrist soothingly.

"You're going to hurt me like that?"

"Not you. People around you."

"It's hurting me as well." Her voice trembled.

Nikolai paused, looking deep into her eyes. His gaze was full of emotion. The mask of a cruel killer had fallen somewhat, revealing a man that looked almost....hurt. The ruthless monster that murdered Dale had pain in his eyes. "If I didn't, you would run away from me."

Angelique couldn't deny that. She would run without turning back. "I don't understand what you want from me. You're doing these awful things to keep me close, to isolate me from my life. Why? For sex?"

"No." He growled. "Because I don't know any better. Because..." He trailed off. His one hand caressed her blond hair. "Because I'm a monster and you're a pure Angel. You'd be better off without me, but I can't let you go again. Not after fate has brought us back together after all these years."

"I don't understand." Angelique felt her heartbeat escalate. She couldn't place her finger on this.

Nikolai read the confusion on her face. "I will keep you until you remember. Until then, you will be mine." Nikolai's fingers trailed the length of her hair. "Every inch of you."

Her eyes widened when he suddenly grasped the back of her skull. His lips crushed into her own roughly. Angelique pushed against his chest in useless protest. It put more fuel into the blazing fire. His tongue slipped into her mouth, deepening the forced kiss. A low growl thundered through his chest. The hand that was holding her wrist trailed down her body, wrapping itself around her thin waist.

He stole away her breath. When he pulled back, she was panting, trembling with anger and sadness.

"This is your punishment for trying to put a knife through my throat." He whispered lowly and then pushed her off his lap. Angelique stumbled, barely managing to hold her balance. "Next time, I won't find the attempt so cute."

Cute!?

"You think me trying to kill you is cute?"

"It is." Slowly, he stood up. His towering body inched closer to her, forcing her to step back until her back way flush against the wall. Nikolai's arms settled besides her head, trapping her. Cold grey eyes stared down at her, any sign of amusement gone. "Next time I will bend you over my knee."

She gulped. "I am not a child."

"You act foolishly like one. Have you forgotten who I am?"

"How could I ever forget." She hissed. "After everything you've done."

Nikolai chuckled, the sound lacking the humor or mirth. His eyes were cold like ice. "Do you expect me to feel guilty?"

"I expect nothing from you." Angelique pushed against his chest. To her surprise, he stepped back. The tears she had been holding back so fervently spilled over, running down her flushed cheeks. "I might have failed to kill you. But one day...someone will succeed." He allowed her to step away, observing calmly how her clenched fists trembled with rage. "And that day, I will celebrate."

Chapter 18

The TV was blaring with the tragic news. A young man, Dale O'Conner, found dead near gas station, brutally beaten by what police assumed were bandits. They had done a decent job making it appear as if he was killed for a petty penny. They took his wallet and damped him in an alleyway for rats to feast on.

A couple of street gangsters were arrested on suspicion of his death. If only they knew...If only she could tell someone why he was dead.

Guilt was eating her alive. It took her apart piece by piece. Amanda had dropped out from the school, claiming she was moving to New York with family. She had promised not to say a word for her own and Angelique's sake. And it was killing her.

Life had become a mere existence in marble walls of Nikolai's mansion. Her father had tried to call a couple of times, but eventually gave up when Angelique didn't pick up. Never in her life she had felt so alone. If that monster's goal was to crush her...to make her suffer....he was succeeding.

"Miss, you have to eat something." Irina's voice cut through the silence.

Angelique didn't respond.

"It's been a week...." The maid carried on, pulling open the thick curtain to let some sunlight into the room.

The sudden brightness made Angelique hiss like she was a bat huddled up in its cave. "Leave me alone."

"I can't do that." Irina stepped towards the bed where the blond woman was cowering under the thick duvets. "Mr. Ivanov wants to see you."

"Tell him I don't want to see him." For a week now he had requested her to eat dinner with him, and gotten her refusal.

"He won't tolerate another excuse, miss..."

"What makes you think I care." Angelique snapped, turning to face away from the obedient servant. Irina's loyalty to that monster made her sick. "How can you work for him? After all the terrible things he has done?"

The mattress dipped. Irina sat down on the edge of the bed. Silence settled between the two. It seemed to stretch on for forever until her voice came to life. "When I was eight, I lost my parents and my home. I had nowhere to go. My foster family only adopted me for money. I was beaten and...." She gulped. "Worse." Her voice was quite, sad. "Mr. Ivanov saved me. Back then he had just taken over the Empire at age of sixteen. He was young and fearsome already." She chuckled. "But he was the only one who offered to help when I was laying near dead on the streets. He took me in. In exchange, I swore my loyalty."

Angelique turned to face Irina. No words of comfort would be enough to express the pity she felt for the young girl. "I'm sorry that happened to you."

Irina shook her head. "Don't be. I have had a good life since then." She smiled. "Back then, he said I reminded him of someone he knew. He does many things wrong. I am not supposed to say this but I think....he doesn't know how to do things differently. He was brought up to be the next leader of Russian mob. I don't know much about his past, but it hasn't been better than mine, I assure you." She paused, timidly glancing down at her hands. "I think he just needs someone...to show him that things can be different." Her eyes trailed to Angelique.

"I don't think someone like him can change." Her hands ballet into fists. "He's a monster."

"Everyone can change, Miss." Irina smiled and then clapped her hands. "But now, please allow me to draw you a bath. With all due respect, you need it badly."

A genuine laugh slipped past her lips. "I suppose." She hadn't gotten out from the bed in far too long. If she didn't plan on playing a skunk, she did need a shower.

Warm water had worked like magic. She felt renewed and like at least part of her sadness had been washed away. Iconic white dress was waiting for her when she stepped out. Nikolai had a thing about seeing her in white. Every evening there was a new snow color dress prepared for her. For the past week she had been stacking them in a pile refusing to wear anything other than pajamas.

Nikolai had given her the privacy she needed, and a part of her still wanted to keep on avoiding him. But something told her that this would lead to no good. They had a running deal, and she still was far from connecting the dots of what he had meant by - Our promise. The words had been intimate, spoken with longing. For her, they only added to confusion and the mystery that kept her locked away in this mansion.

A hulking SUV was waiting outside. Dog held the door open, his expression twisted into a fearsome scowl. No one said a word where it would take her. To think that she would've grown numb to fear by now. No. Her heart was beating louder than the roar of engine.

Perhaps he had finally made up his mind about getting rid of her.

I tried to kill him after all. Angelique mused.

Her short fingernails clawed at her legs nervously, leaving behind fading red marks. The mansion disappeared in distance. The suspense was killing her. There was no use asking questions. By now she knew better than to try. Dog and his men only responded to Nikolai, and he was nowhere in sight.

A torturous hour later, the car finally came to a halt by a beach. The briny air kissed along her cheeks and wind whipped at her long hair. Wild waves banged against the rocky shore. She would've payed more attention to the beauty of this place, if her attention wouldn't be stolen by a dark figure in distance.

Nikolai stood with his arms stuffed in front packets of his trousers, watching her with cold grey eyes.

The tension in her built sky high. The looming sensation of dread got her breath to hitch.

"Angel." He accosted, his gaze following her every step. His men stayed behind, smoking and chatting among themselves without paying attention to the two of them. Except for Dog, his eyes were trained on Angelique's back, serving to unsettle her further.

"What is this about?" She inquired.

"Care to take a walk?" It wasn't really an offer. The warmth of his large hand settling on the small of her back made her nerves tingle with a new kind of nervous.

She fell into the step besides him, trying not to shiver from the biting cold of the wind. "Am I next to feast with the fish?" Bitter humor playing through her voice. She wouldn't be too surprised if he chose to drown her in the cold water, watch the life fade from her eyes. He was vicious enough to lure her into false sense of security and then strike when she expected it the least.

"It would be an awful waste of a beautiful woman." He huffed out a dry sounding laugh, deep and rough as the man himself. Nikolai's hand trailed from her back to pull off his suit jacket. With a swift motion he dropped it over her slender shoulders."Don't get cold." He said simply, unaffected by the harsh wind.

The large jacket was warm against her skin. Angelique felt her cheeks heat. The smell of his cologne seeped into her senses. He was galant for a mobster, that was for sure.

Don't let a kind gesture fog up your thoughts. She scolded herself. I can't let own my guard. He a monster. Be brave.

"Why am I here?" She demanded.

"To walk."

Angelique frowned. "You expect me to believe that?"

"Yes." Nikolai stated simply. "You didn't leave your room for a week. You look sickly pale." He glanced down at her. "You needed sun."

If she would be sitting, she would've fallen from the chair, utterly baffled.

Is he playing the caring friend now!?

Anger welled up in her veins. "Is this some sort of attempt at an apology? Is this it?" Her voice grew fierce with wrath. "You think I will forgive you everything you did after a walk by the beach!? If so-"

"I'm not apologizing." He interrupted her. "That kid touched what belongs to me."

The two of them came to a stop. At this point she was seeing red. "When are you going to stop treating me like I fucking belong to you!?" She didn't care if she was yelling or cursing. Angelique was too pissed off to care. All the built-up frustrations went spilling over. Without thinking, she grabbed his hand, leading it to her chest. "Feel that!? It's called a heart."

Nikolai's eyebrows raised with shock. He didn't make a move to pull his hand away. He simply stared at it, feeling her pulse go ramped underneath the silky skin.

"I am a person, not your possession." Angelique looked into his eyes. He could no longer pretend to be indifferent.

She saw the emotion swirling under the grey irises, even if he chose to remain silent.

Her fingers tightened around his wrist. His pulse was racing.

"I-" He begun.

BANG!

The air shuttered. The oxygen swelled in her lungs, stuck there with no other purpose than to choke her. The loud noise made her ears ring.

Slowly, her gaze trailed from Nikolai to a stain on her shoulder. It hadn't been there before. It was wet and dark, and kept growing bigger. Her shaky fingers released his wrist, swiping up the ruby liquid that now seeped out from a dark hole in her flesh.

Blood.

And then came the surge of pain, so powerful it had her knees buckling. It spread through her entire body, burning.

Two strong arms caught her falling body just as another bang followed the first. And then came more, but she no longer registered the noise. Her legs no longer touched the ground, and she was enveloped in something warm. It held her close.

He held her close.

"Stay awake." Nikolai whispered. "Angel, stay the fuck awake!" Angelique heard his deep voice amongst the yelling and thundering orders. Her head lolled back against his broad shoulder, her eyes closing.

Before she caved into consciousness she heard something that made her heart jump. Perhaps it had been the trick her her tired mind. An illusion. But she heard him whisper.

"Forgive me, Angelique."

Chapter 19

Pain is merciless - capable of breaking and shattering the strongest. It sears through the body like a storm, sweeping away the sane thoughts, taking everything that is good and twisting it against you.

It makes you beg not to feel.

Her eyes opened to white ceiling and distant cracking of fire. The light glow danced at the side of her vision. Angelique had been slipping in and out of unconsciousness. First time she awoke was in a car. She was laid out on the backseat, her head cradled by warm, strong embrace. The second time, everything was more blurry. There were a lot of white, blinding lights and mix of voices she didn't recognize. She was being rushed to somewhere and she could clearly remember a man in medical mask peering down at her.

And the third time was now. The panic and commotion was gone. There was only the distant sound of fire blazing across the room.

Her mouth felt dry and her body was stiff.

"What happened?" The raspy whisper pushed past her chapped lips. She wasn't sure if anyone heard it, or if there was anyone in the room with her in the first place.

Then there was shuffling from other side of the room, followed by heavy thumping of footsteps. Dazed, she followed the source of the sound. A tall, huge man approached the bed, his movements a tad awkward, like the room was spinning and he was just barely keeping from toppling over.

"Angel." His voice was gruff, thick with accent. The man stumbled into her sight, glazed over grey eyes staring down at her feeble form. Nikolai slumped down on the bed, careful not to bump against her. An empty whiskey bottle was clutched in his one hand, bits of amber drink swiveling at the bottom.

He's dead drunk. She noted. This was the first time she had seen Nikolai, the fearsome mafia leader come unhinged. Angelique had seen him drink many times, but never get bombed.

"What happened?" The young woman repeated, getting used to the dryness in her throat. "My...shoulder hurts."

"You got shot."

"Shot?" Her voice broke off into a croak.

"I wasn't careful." Nikolai slurred, staring down at her pale face. "It was a sniper. The bullet was meant for me, but got you instead." Slowly he reached out to tuck a loose strand behind her ear. He was being so gentle that this might as well be a dream. "It struck your shoulder." He explained, "Doctors said it's flesh wound."

Hurts anyway.

"I see..." She wasn't certain how to react to this. "How long...was I out?"

"Two days."

Nikolai inched closer when she made a move to sit up. "Don't." He growled. Even when tipsy, his voice rung with the type of authority that didn't allow to disobey.

She winced, hand coming up to caress the bandage wrapped around her shoulder and chest area. "Do you know who did it?"

"Not yet." His eyes blackened dangerously. "But when I will, God better have mercy on them."

Angelique swallowed. "I need-" Before she could finish the sentence, Nikolai had already reached for a glass of water set on the nightstand. His large hand slid under her head. Carefully he put the glass to her lips. The water soothed her dry throat. She gulped it down hungrily.

"Thank you." She murmured when he pulled the empty glass back. "Why are you here?" Angelique blurt out. The question had been bouncing back and forth in her head. "Irina could've helped me."

"I refuse to leave you alone until I find who harmed you." His voice was serious, and his words final. There was no changing his mind no matter what she said.

"So overprotective." The silent chuckle turned into a cough.

Who knew being shot is this awful?

"You should sleep." Nikolai caressed her golden locks, his rough fingers undoing the knots gently. "I will stay here and watch over you."

He begun to move away, stopping abruptly when she caught him by the edge of his sleeve. "Don't." Angelique was this desperate for comfort, to the point where lines between good and evil blurred. Maybe it was his vulnerable side that made her want him to stay, or maybe it was become of whatever meds they gave her. For once she didn't want to be alone, even if only one to keep her company was equivalent to devil himself.

Nikolai sat back down without a word. He wasn't a man to quip and crack jokes about peoples weaknesses. Before she might've wished he was, it would make the come-backs easier, but for now she was thankful for his silent nature.

The young woman soaked in the calm moment, savoring it like fine wine before she would crash it to shreds. She might be dazed from her injury, but her mind was still sharp, and her nature - curious. "You once told me that all women are dirty. Why do you think that?" She asked, gazing up at him through long lashes.

"Because they are." Nikolai glared at an empty space be-sides her head. "They are like my mother. All of them, ex-cept for you." Maybe it was alcohol speaking. Certainly, he wouldn't be telling her this otherwise.

Angelique remained silent, waiting for him to continue.

He didn't.

"What makes me different." She pressed. A nagging part of her wanted - no - needed to know more about him. What made him the way he was? What triggered all the cruel things he did? Why did he hate women? So many questions and so little chances of getting answers. This was one of those chances. No way she's letting it slide.

"You think I don't know what you're doing, Angel?" His harsh gaze zeroed in on her. "I am not that drunk."

"I want to know more about you." She was not about to give up.

Silence settled and then he sighed. Her eyes widened when he suddenly begun to take his shirt off.

"What are you doing-"

"You wanted to know." He stated simply, tossing the shirt aside. "My mother was pathetic and nasty woman, trapped in arranged marriage with my father." He started, "She hated me because I was his son. A part of him." Gently, he took ahold of her hand, bringing it to his muscular chest.

Under layers of ink were small scabs of healed over wounds. "He only needed her for a heir. When I was born, he no longer bothered to hide his affairs, which made her hate me even more." Cigarette burns. Countless of them littered his chest and taunt abdomen.

"She did that to you..."

"She did." He confirmed. "And worse. The older I got, the more abuse she felt obliged to inflict." His tone was somber. He lead her hand to scars across his ribs.

Angelique gulped. She never expected to feel pity for the man who took away her freedom and killed her friend. And yet, she did.

"She laughed when I was crying." Nikolai had distant look in his eyes. It oozed deep rooted hate. His grip on her hand tightened to near bruising before he came to, and let her hand drop. "I killed her when I was sixteen."

Her breath hitched. He said it with no emotions, like it was a reasonable thing to do. But she didn't blame him, not after what that woman did to him.

"You think I am an even bigger monster now, don't you." His smile was chilling to the bone. It got her blood to freeze in her veins.

"No." She said after a pause. "You are a monster, but I don't think this makes you worse. I could never understand what you went through. What was done to you is awful. And I don't blame you for what you did..."

He studied her expression, searching for lies. He found none. Nikolai's face relaxed into something she hadn't seen before. He smiled. "You're too good for this world, Angel. Too good for me..." He said lowly.

Nikolai leaned closer until she could smell the alcohol in his breath. She didn't mind.

When he gazed at her like this, it became harder to think of him as the evil of the world. The chips in his mask had split, and it had fallen, revealing a broken man underneath. They gazed into each others eyes, their breaths mingling.

Her lips parted. No words came out. No words were needed to be said. Instead she lifted her head and their lips met.

The world went crushing around them. For all she cared, it could turn to ashes. For the first time she kissed him with passion. Perhaps she would come to regret this, but that was trouble for tomorrow.

Her hand caressed under his defined cheekbone, feeling the smooth skin move under the pads of her fingers. Nikolai groaned with her touch, deepening their kiss.

Neither pulled away, and both needed more.

Chapter 20

The kiss took her breath away - deep and perhaps a bit sloppy. She didn't care. His tongue explored her mouth with lustful vigor, and she couldn't stop the butterflies from swirling in her core. Her small arms wrapped around his broad shoulders, fingers running through the thick messy locks of his hair. They had grown longer since they first met. She loved the wild look on him.

Nikolai was first to pull back, panting. "You're hurt." He rasped, pure, scalding heat dancing in his eyes. Desire. Want. Need. She couldn't begin to name all the things she was seeing. Among them all, concern - as clear as day.

This was a good moment to pull back and claim this was a mistake, a heat of the moment inspired by his drunken state and meds. But she didn't. Instead, "I'll be fine." She breathed.

It was all the permission he needed. They had been intimate before. She did sell her virginity to him after all, but back then it was like sealing a business deal. He was cold and merciless. Now his touch was feathery light like he was afraid to break her.

His large, carouse hand trailed from her cheek, down her exposed neck and past the bandages around her chest. Her toes curled. The blanket dragged down her body excruciatingly slowly. He was taking in every inch of her.

Nikolai trailed his fingers down her abdomen, curling them around the edge of her sweatpants. "You're a very beautiful woman." He whispered, and then, yanked the pants past her hips and down her slender legs, all while being careful not to hurt her.

"So beautiful." He leaned over her, planting another deep kiss on her lips. It made her all but soaked. Somewhere in the back of her head the sane part of her was hissing of how wrong this was, but the second his long fingers caressed her over her wet underwear, none of those thoughts had any weight to them anymore.

Angelique gasped. He pushed her panties to the side, stroking her wet folds lightly. The perfect torture. "Please..." She whined, words pouring past her lips before she could stop them. "More."

Nikolai grinned, a wave of satisfaction coursing through him with the simple plead. "Please what?" He was being cruel in the best way possible. Another stroke of his fingers and her hips bucked against his hand. "Say it, Angel." He demanded.

Damn. He looked like a hungry wolf toying with his innocent prey. And he enjoyed it. Sadist.

"I want you." She clarified through heavy breaths. Her shoulder was beginning to ache, but somehow it only added to the general pleasure.

A ripping sound echoed through the room. With a swift move he had her panties torn from her body, leaving her completely naked aside the bandage. A wolflike growl rumbled through his chest. Nikolai took a moment to look over her, then his lips were once again on hers. He kissed downward, sucking on her neck, skipping past the bandage and going lower.

"Wait-" She wanted to protest, unsure what he was going for. But the hand she had extended to stop him was quickly grabbed and position in his hair.

"Relax." The single word order spread an ache of need between her thighs. Her fingers pulled at his thick locks, unconfined moan slipping past her lips, when his lips dipped between her legs. He teased her, kissing everywhere but where she wanted him to. Only when she couldn't take it anymore, his tongue found the sensitive bundle of nerves.

Angelique nearly came from the first touch. No one had done this to her before. The strong sensations of pleasure made her mind turn utterly blank. "Nikolai." She breathed his name when his tongue flicked against her.

Seconds later orgasm hit her harder than a battering ram. The pain in her shoulder no longer mattered. She tensed, her toes curled and her fingers nearly ripped his hair out.

The waves of pleasure shook through her again and again. Nikolai didn't pull back until the sensation became too much to take. She whined, and he lifted his head, wiping his mouth with the back of his hand, devilish look in his eyes.

God, why the hell is he so sexy?

She could clearly see the massive bulge in his pants, demanding to be released from its confinement. Angelique felt exhausted and content, but it wasn't nearly enough to ease the sensation of want.

Nikolai spread her legs, settling his hips between them. "Are you sure?"

Since when did he ask for her consent? Since now, apparently.

Angelique nodded. "Gently." She still feared the pain she felt the first time they did this. He had fucked her raw. Something about the way he looked at her this time though, told her things were far different than they were.

"Gentle." Nikolai mumbled in agreement, undoing his trousers. His erection stood tall, thick vein that run along its length pulsating with need.

He pressed a gentle kiss on her lips. She could taste herself on his mouth, and it spared a new kind of desire within her. Nikolai propped himself up on one hand while the other angled the shaft to her entrance.

Slowly, he thrust forwards.

His massive length spread her walls, settling deeper and deeper until he was all the way inside. Breathless moan left her lips. It was a tight fit, but the sensation was far more enjoyable than it was the first time they had sex. This time Nikolai was being careful. Gentle even.

Both of his arms settled on either side of her. With a low groan, he pulled back and thrust back in. His rugged breaths brushed against the nape of her neck. "Fuck." He growled, fingers gripping the sheets to keep himself from being rough.

Angelique clawed at his broad, tattooed back, wincing whenever she moved her bad arm too much. He was holding back for her sake. Nikolai wasn't a man that made love. He fucked. But now, he was gentle, the movement of his hips slow and controlled. His length filled her up entirely, hitting the place inside her that made her want to scream every time.

"Angel..." He rasped a warning. He was close. She was as well. Couple thrusts later, he dipped her over the sweet edge. Her nails dug into his back, head lolling back and eyes rolling. It was intense, prolonged by his measured movements.

Nikolai made sure she rode off her orgasm, his rhythm picking up ever so slightly as she convulsed around him, breathing out his name.

Angelique felt him stiffen inside he. He pulled out in haste. White seed sputtered across her flat stomach, his low growls echoing through the room.

Both of them were left breathing hard, staring at each other in awe.

She could hardly believe what had just happened. When the blind passion subsided, her chest clenched with guilt.

Shit, what the hell did I do?

You had sex with a monster. And you enjoyed it. The same voice in the back of her head responded.

Her eyes closed.

Holy fuck...I did, didn't I?

Chapter 21

When her eyes peeled open the next morning, the sheets besides her were cold. His masculine scent lingered on the pillow she clutched to her chest. The sun was high in the sky, its merciless bright rays blazing down at her through the gaps in curtains.

With a groan, Angelique rolled over. Her shoulder was killing her, much like the settling realization that she had willingly allowed Nikolai between her legs. And enjoyed it immensely.

God.

She groaned into the pillow. It had been a moment of weakness. He was vulnerable, and to be frank, also drunk, and very handsome. The disheveled hair, the unbuttoned shirt, the soft grey eyes. Damn, he got her good.

He had been so gentle, nothing like the mob boss she knew him to be.

And apparently it's all It takes for me to give in.

She wanted to scream her lungs out. In a single night the man she hated - the guy that had totally ruined her life - had charmed her into sleeping with him. Literally.

Angelique glanced at the empty space besides her. They had passed out together, his heavy arm draped across her waist. It had been so comforting and warm to sleep in his embrace.

"You moron." She scolded herself.

The ache in her shoulder intensified. For once she was thankful to pain. It took her mind off of the hunky wolf.

Groaning, Angelique slumped back into the covers. Was it supposed to hurt this much?

Duah. You got shot, genius.

The pain meds had ran their course and she was left writhing in agony. It was fucking bad. Cold sweat coated her skin and the more she moved the worst the pain got, robbing her of senses. She didn't even hear when the door cracked open.

"Angel." A cool hand suddenly settled on her forehead. "You're burning up." Familiar deep voice stated, cursing lowly. "Get a doctor in here! Stat! "

Her eyes had grown heavy again. Too heavy to open. Her blurred mind registered that the booming voice belonged to Nikolai. He was saying something in Russian. If she more strength, she would scold him for saying things she didn't understand. His voice sounded rougher when he spoke his native tongue, barking orders left and right. Only distantly she heard other people shuffle inside the room.

She felt searing pain and his cold hand stroking her hair before everything slipped back into pitch black.

Angelique awoke when the sun had dipped below the horizon. The fire was once again casting the orange glow across the room, and a lamp was lit up on the nightstand besides her.

"Finally, you're awake." Irina's worried voice echoed. "How are you feeling?" The woman sat forwards on the bed, genuine concern printed on her face.

"Like crap."

Irina forced a chuckle. "You got feverish. Doctors said you need to rest and drink a lot of water."

"Where is..." She looked around the room, hoping to see the familiar tall figure.

As if to read her mind, Irina answered, "Mr. Ivanov is at the meeting. They are trying to figure out who attacked you. Attempt at his life is a serious crime." Her voice dropped to a softer tone, "He hasn't left your side until now. I was asked to look after you while he's gone." She smiled. "You truly mean a lot to him."

"I'm just his possession." Angelique admitted bitterly.

"I don't think so." Irina argued, "He has changed since he met you. I can't really put my finger on it, but..." She trailed off. "Sorry, it's not my place to say."

"No. Please do tell me." The blond woman instead weakly.

The maid glanced around the room and leaned in closer as if she was about to tell her a top secret. "I think you mean more to him then his Empire. I have never seen him get worried, but when you got the fever, he was...frantic. He even threatened to kill the doctor if he didn't help you. I have never seen him like that."

After that she barely saw Nikolai. Mainly because she was sleeping most of the time. Angelique felt his presents a couple of times, holding her hand or caressing her blond hair. Someone was always by her side, seeing to her needs. A doctor came three times a day to check up on the wound.

A week rolled by with her lounging in the large bed, recovering. Nikolai had even called the school for her, telling them she had a flu.

Each day it was getting harder and harder to lay around and do nothing but watch Netflix.

Finally, she couldn't take it anymore.

Angelique slipped out from the comfort of the bed, stretching the best she could not to pull on her stitches. Doctor had said he would remove them soon, and that everything looked like it was healing up neatly. Of course, he had instructed her to stay bed ridden, but her limbs were begging her to move.

Irina had left to get lunch despite Angelique insisting that she could do it herself. This gave her an excellent opportunity to walk around without being scolded like a kid. If she spent another day in that damned bed, she would die. At least that's what it felt like.

Dressed in grey sweatpants and simple white t-shirt, Angelique sauntered out from the room. A sigh of relief tumbled past her lips when she saw no one guarding the room.

Thank all Gods and Superman.

With quiet steps, she sneaked across the hallway, alert at all times. She was a woman with an agenda. The massive garden outside the mansion was particularly calling her name. Fresh, crisp air. She couldn't think of anything she needed more than that.

"We have a mole."

Her steps came to a sudden halt in front of large door. Nikolai's office.

"Who is it?"

"We don't know yet."

"Then find out." Male voices came from the other side, one of them belonging to the big man himself. She shuddered at the sound of his deep baritone. Angelique knew that she had to kick things into gear if she wanted to reach the garden in one piece. But her legs had turned to heavy stones. They were clearly talking about who attacked her.

"I want to deal with that scum myself." Nikolai's voice boomed.

"Certainly. We are doing our best-" Another man said.

"Do better. Or I will make sure to deal with you next."

She gulped. When he held her to his muscular body, it was easy to forget what he was truly capable of. That he was the head of Russian mafia. Not the boss you'd want to work for.

Suddenly the door flew open in her face. Angelique barely managed to avoid it from hitting her straight in the face. Her body froze. All eyes were on her. Three men she wasn't familiar with stood in the room. Dog was there as well, smoking a cigarette by the window.

Nikolai sat at his desk, brooding. His sharp grey eyes pinned her down with a single glance.

Fuck-

"Why aren't you in the bed?" His tone could freeze over Africa.

"I..." Angelique cleared her throat. Gathering up her courage, she entered the office, very much aware of all the gangsters staring at her like they were about to pull guns on her ass. "I couldn't sleep anymore. I want to know what's going on."

His eyes narrowed dangerously. "Go back to bed. This is an order, Angel."

She returned his glare. "I will be sick from sleeping. I am sick of that room. I won't leave until you tell me what is going on." Speak of boost of courage. Or stupidity. They could simply make her go back, and regret her words later. She was almost expecting it to happen by the way everyone was staring at her.

"Out." Nikolai ordered, side-glancing at his men. None protested, even if they did look baffled that it wasn't her being tossed out from the office. The door clicked shut, leaving them alone.

"I would punish you for this if you weren't hurt." Nikolai leaned back into his chair, the sharpness in his gaze easing off somewhat. "What do you want to know, Angel?"

Wow. He actually won't kick me out.

Smiling, she sat down on the chair across from him. "I want to know what you know."

"That's not much then."

"Still better than suspense."

A deep hum rumbled through his chest. "We're suspecting it could be someone that...works for me." The low growl in his voice hinted towards how he felt about being betrayed by his own men. A shiver went down her spine. To think what would happen when he figured out who the culprit was... "For now, we can't trust anyone."

"Has something like this happened before?"

"More often than you think." He grumbled. "Those petty turn-coats are loyal only to cash. If someone payed them to kill me, they would without hesitating."

She felt a lump form in her throat. The bullet didn't hit the right target. Which means, it could happen again.

"It's not a professional though." Nikolai mused.

"Why do you think that?" Everyone in this mansion besides cooks and Irina looked like pro killers. They wouldn't blink before firing off a bullet to someones head.

"If it was, I would've been dead." He stated. "And you would too."

That makes sense.

"What can we do?" They couldn't just wait for that sloppy gangster to try again!

Nikolai frowned. "Leave that up to me." He leaned forwards, settling his arms on the desk. "For now, however..." An evil glimmer appeared in his eyes. "I have a more pressing matter of chaining a certain girl to the bed."

Chapter 22

Things had changed since the night they spend snuggling under the covers, if ever so slightly. Nikolai had made it his personal mission to keep her in the bed until she made a full recovery. Though, at times it did involve him staying in the bed with her. The mask of ruthless leader he wore slipped away whenever they were alone.

Every day revealed a new side of him. That he was capable of empathy, kindness, integrity. Angelique had shared her passion for dance, and he taught her how to play chess. They had joked and laughed like two normal human beings. Whatever she might request of him, he saw to carrying it out.

But it wasn't enough to make her forget or to forgive.

The dark, malicious side of him still existed, strong and dominant. She saw it flickering beneath his gaze, eating away the kindness she now knew he was capable of.

Nikolai didn't conduct business in front of her. But every time he came home late with his knuckles bruised and his suit stained by ruby red blood, it served to remind her who he really was. A monster. Even if at times she tricked herself into thinking otherwise.

"What's on your mind, Angel?" Nikolai's deep voice cut through the fragile trail of thoughts. His fingers stroked up and down her bare back. Her cheek was pressed against his tattooed chest, feeling the thumping heartbeat underneath. A small reminder that he did have a heart.

"Nothing." She responded.

His eyes narrowed. "It's not nothing. Don't hide things from me." Demand rung clear in his tone. It was unsettling how easily he could see into her mind.

Like an open book.

Angelique sighed, tilting her chin up to look into his grey irises. "I was just wondering..." She sucked in a deep breath. "Have you ever considered quitting this business?"

Nikolai tensed. The hand stroking her back stopped. "What is this about?" The warning in his voice was chilling. It sent an unpleasant shiver down her spine.

Slowly, she sat up to get a proper look at his face. "Would you ever quit the mafia?" Something bloomed between them for a while now - more than just this messed up game he had started or sex, or a rush or physical desire. Something stronger and far more demanding than that.

She feared the emotion, and refused to name it.

It's not possible to feel that towards a monster.

"There's a life out there without...killing." She continued.

"Not for me." Nikolai countered. "You should know better than anyone. Mafia is what I am. It's my life."

"It could be different-"

"Stop it." He stood up, cutting the conversation to the root. "We are not having this conversation."

"We should." Angelique stressed. "There is more to you than this! I've seen it!"

"You've seen nothing!" He snapped, feral look in his eyes, Nikolai picking up his scattered clothes. He refused to even glance her way as he got dressed.

The young woman was far from done talking. He couldn't avoid this conversation for forever. "Don't give me that." She hissed.

The mask was back on, his features made of stone and eyes icy. Everything she had built and revealed during past weeks was shuttered and no longer of importance - just because she asked the simple question.

"If I meant anything to you. You would stop and listen! Fucking look at me for once!"

Nikolai paused, half dressed. His cold, narrowed eyes landed on her form. The look he gave her, could send the strongest men to their knees.

Angelique gathered the blanket around her naked body. She walked up to him. "It's not too late to change." The young woman ignored the tic in his jaw. Muscles taunt, he looked ready snap. Rip her to shreds. But she couldn't turn back from this. "Would you do it...for me?"

The silence was heavy. Suffocating.

"I...There's this girl working at your club. Her name is Zoe." She spoke when he didn't respond. "If you help her start over, I would-"

"No." The sharp word cut through her like a knife through butter. Her breath hitched.

Nikolai tilted up her chin, glaring down at her. "You're forgetting your place, Angel. I have always been a bad man, and I will always be. For your own sake, I wouldn't forget that." His grip tightened, becoming painful. "I might've told you a thing or two about my past. That doesn't mean you know anything about me. It doesn't mean that anything has changed."

He let go of her jaw, facing away from her. Like he couldn't stand to look at her. "I won't be here for dinner." The door slammed behind him with an echoing bang.

Her knees buckled. Angelique sunk onto the ground, teeth grit.

You naive fool...

Tears streamed down her pale cheeks. A couple of nights spent in bliss had convinced her she could see a man behind the monster. She was wrong. So fucking wrong. Her chest felt tight.

Nikolai didn't bend to manipulation, even if she didn't think of it as such. All she had ever desired was for this nightmare to be over. But it wasn't. And unless she took things in her own hands, nothing really would change.

Her hands balled into white-knuckled fists.

Take things into my own hands.

Hours later, sun dipped below the horizon. The large mansion was eerie silent. Half of the staff was gone and her flimsy plan was set into motion. Hot anger boiling in her veins and determination working her steps for her, Angelique sneaked out from her room.

She would pay for this. Perhaps.

The young woman was fed up with this situation. She was not just his pretty doll. Once Angelique had given Zoe a promise. And she planned to keep it, with or without his help.

The door to Nikolai's office was locked when she tried the handle.

Shit. Plan B.

She pulled a bobby pin from her pocket. Another useful thing her good-for-nothing father had done was teach her how to pick locks. When she was a kid, he kept losing the keys to their house in his drunken stupor. She did this more than she liked to admit. For once her dad's bad drinking habit had produced something good.

Taking a quick glance around, she twisted the bobby-pin and inserted it into the lock. A moment of tinkering later, satisfying click echoed through the hall.

Perfect.

The door cracked open. A proud smile tugged onto her lips. She was sneaking into Mob boss office in a mansion guarded so well, it put the White House to shame. Not many could claim doing those things.

With quite steps, she sauntered inside. Angelique had to act fast. Hurriedly, she went up to the massive mahogany desk set in middle of the room. The young woman made sure not to disturb a single piece of paper or pen. Her delicate hands rampaged through his drawers, her heart drumming in her ears.

Finally!

The last drawer at the very bottom revealed the jackpot. A receipt book in thick leather covers, well used at that. To think she would ever try a hand in fraud. Well, the owner of this book had done worse. Might as well. Bad things justified by a good cause.

Angelique flipped through the book. Lady Luck was on her side. One of the receipt's had his signature on it, and a decent number hand-written on a dotted line. The receiver of this would be very happy.

Carefully, she ripped the receipt from the book. So far, her plan was a sparkling success. The hardest part was yet to come however. She had to get to the club.

Thump! Thump!

Just as she was about to put the book back in its place, heavy footsteps echoed down the hall.

Her heart plummeted.

Every single curse word under the sun ran through her mind. As quickly and quietly as she could, Angelique sunk beneath the desk, pulling her knees to her chest.

The footsteps grew louder, approaching the office door she had left hanging ajar.

Angelique swallowed, her face twisted in utter horror when the steady thumping paused by the door. Then the loud crack of it opening followed by someone entering the office.

Doomed. I am so doomed.

Chapter 23

Two shiny black loafers caught the dim moonlight seeping from the large window. The silent tap of flat sole against the lush carpet made her heartbeat spike.

Angelique held her breath, pushing herself so far into shadows, she wished she could melt into them, become part of the decor on the wooden desk.

"I know you're here." An accent rich voice stated. "Come out." The vicious tone this man used rung crips and clear. The message was unmistakable, 'Come out and you'll be a goner.' Her gut twisted at the thought. No one would care why she had broken into Nikolai's office. She was here, and that was enough to behead her.

They wouldn't give two shits about her being their boss favorite. It disgusted her to think that, but she could hardly deny it. She was his mistress of sorts. Think! Damn it, Angelique, Think!

"Show yourself!" The owner of the expensive shoes grew far more agitated by every passing second. He was closing in on the desk.

Think!

What if he has a gun? I'll be dead! No, think of something, woman!

Angelique sucked in a large gulp of air. There was only one thing she could do. He was seconds away from spotting her, and then her leverage would be gone. And that refined plan was to....

Run!

As if fire had been sat under her ass, Angelique bolted from her hiding spot behind the desk. The guard barely had the time to react. "Stop!" He roared as the young woman swooshed past him. The man reached for his hostler-

BANG!

The massive door slammed in his face. The lock she had successfully picked fell back into place with a click, locking the intruder inside the office. His fists banged against the wood, shouting for her to open the door.

Like hell. And let him shoot me? No way.

Angelique smirked hauntingly. Damn, she actually had pulled that off? She should've considered secret agent career after all. Agility that came with years of dancing had saved the day. Her shoulder ached with dull pain, reminding her that she had been shot once. No way in hell she was going through that ever again.

The young woman fell into a light jog. Sooner or later someone would hear the guard yelling. She had to leave before that happens.

Gathering up remains of courage, she carried on. One thing she had learned from watching gangsters was that even if you were scared shit-less, you had to keep your head high and someone might buy it.

Row of black cars was parked in front of the massive mansion. She slowed down her jog, straightened her form and tilted her chin up. Head high, voice cold. You can do this.

Three men stood outside, smoking and chatting among themselves. Three pairs of sharp eyes snapped towards her the second she waltzed out from the mansion.

"I need someone to take me to the club." Angelique demanded, disregarding the ball of stress in her throat. For them, she wasn't the scared girl going against Nikolai. No. She was the mafia princess. His angel. If they disobeyed, their boss would have their guts decorating the walls of some rotten warehouse.

She just had to establish the thought in their heads, and prey that Nikolai hadn't given them a direct order not to let her wander outside the mansion.

The three men exchanged a look. They were hesitating. Not good.

"Well?" Angelique put on the best glare she could muster. "Take me to the club or I will tell Nikolai you disobeyed his orders. We don't want that to happen, do we, boys?" Wow. She actually managed to keep her ice queen act together.

She would pat her own shoulder if it wouldn't destroy her image.

One of the trio shuffled towards a black car. "Right away, miss." He opened the door for her, dropping his cigarette on an instant.

It fucking worked!

She could hardly believe her own eyes. The second she had settled inside the car, a proud smile spread on her lips. She just had to finish this up before Nikolai got back from whatever business he was on, and then deny leaving the mansion all together.

A good hour or so later, the car parked in front of the all too familiar club. Ages had rolled by since she was last there. She had almost forgotten the awful vibe it gave off. So much had happened since she first took a step inside this establishment, it could drive just about anyone insane.

The club was swarmed by people. It was a Friday night and she could hear the demands for drinks all the way from outside. The music pounded loudly from within. She had underestimated how stressful this would be.

Walking past a puking woman and a couple making out against the wall outside the club, Angelique headed straight for the back door - a quickest way to the changing rooms. Nothing had changed since she was last there. The same ruby red halls. Secretive VIP rooms where lap dances took place. And hollers of horny clients demanding whoever was on the stage to strip.

The memories alone made her shudder. Had she chosen not to sell her virginity, she would still be stuck there, among the cigarette smoke and grabby hands.

Yuck.

She opened the door to the changing room, spotting the usual crowd there. Jess was sitting cross-legged by the brightly lit mirror, applying jungle red lipstick to her plump lips. Lila was putting on the massive stilettos when her big eyes landed on the figure standing at the door.

Both women froze.

"Angel?!" Jess nearly shouted, painted eyebrows shooting upwards in shock. "What the actual- You're back?"

Lila gaped, staring at her as if she was a ghost.

"Where is Zoe?" Angelique asked, her voice far from timid. She had come here for her friend, and would not leave until she saw her.

The two other women looked taken aback by her tone. "She's dancing..." Jess replied, hesitant. The question was written all over her face before she even asked it. "What the hell happened to you? You just disappeared. No one told us anything."

"Isn't it obvious?" Lila snorted. "She switched careers from stripping to warming beds. What happened, Angel? He kicked you out?"

Angelique frowned. "Still a bitch, I see." Some things really didn't change. "I came here to see Zoe.-" Before she could finish the sentence the door flew open from behind her.

Zoe burst inside the room, looking dog tired and sweaty. Her red hair had lost their glow, and her eyes were bloodshot under the heavy make up. That was far from the worst part. Under the thick layer of foundation were obvious lines of a huge bruise. Her entire left cheek was swollen and her movements were somewhat stiff with pain. Someone had used her as a punching bag.

Angelique stared in shock. She had never seen her in this kind of state. It was awful!

"Angel..." Zoe paused at the door, her green eyes widening. "What...you're here?" She looked baffled.

Before the blond woman could respond or even formulate a question, Zoe threw her arms around her in a tight hug. "My god...I thought they took you. I thought-" She was shaking.

Hesitantly Angelique wrapped her arms around her friend, careful not to touch the battered flesh. "I came to see you." She finally managed to say, pulling back slightly. "What happened to you?"

The red head's face dropped, growing gloom. The cheerful spark from her eyes was gone. "Let's talk somewhere more private." Angelique followed Zoe out from the changing room where Jess and Lila couldn't hear them.

"First, tell me what the hell happened to you." Zoe insisted the second she had made sure no one was around to listen.

Angelique wasn't sure where to begin. "I...made a deal with Nikolai." She begun. "I don't have much time, so I can't tell you much. All you must know is that I'm fine. He's treating me good."

Zoe looked like she didn't believe a single word. "I find that hard to believe." She admitted. "Nikolai is-"

"I'm well aware. Believe me." In fact, she knew better than anyone who he was. She had the first row seat to the awful things he did. But she was also the only one to witness his caring side. "It's not what I came here to talk about. What did they do to you?" Genuine concern seeped into her voice.

Zoe hung her head. "Yesterday's client was a sadist. He was into beating women-" She choked on her own words. Angelique felt her stomach drop. She had gone through the same once. The memory alone made her stomach twist with nausea. "And that's not the worst part..." She swallowed. "I think I'm...pregnant."

Holy shit!

"I haven't had my period this moth." Zoe broken down, sobbing. "I am knocked up by one of them and I can't-"

Angelique pulled her into a hug, letting the woman sob into her hair. "My God..." She couldn't help the gush. "Do you want to get rid of it?"

"No." Zoe cried, pulling back to look at her friend. "I have always wanted a family...But I'm a stripper. I can't rise a kid. I need to get rid of it."

"Maybe you don't." This was better time than any to reveal why she was here. Angelique pulled out the check from her pocket, handing it to Zoe.

"What is this?" Her green eyes fell on the sum written down on the piece of paper, her jaw going slack. "Angel, what is this?" She questioned breathlessly.

"I promised you once that I will find a way to get you out. I am keeping that promise."

"But-"

"It's your new life. And the life for your kid. It's not much, but it's a start. Buy ticket to New York. I have a friend there. Her name is Amanda. She won't refuse to help you." Angelique explained, pushing another piece of paper with Amanda's number into Zoe's hand.

"I can't..."

"You must." Angelique insisted. Her tone was firm. No was not an answer she was willing to accept. Not after everything she did to get that receipt.

Zoe fell silent, staring dumbfounded at the piece of paper that held her future. The spark of joy returned in her bright green eyes and a genuine smile stretched onto her red lips. "You have changed." She said. "This angel has grown a pair of horns and lost the halo. You have grown." The red-head grinned. "You have him wrapped around your little finger, don't you?"

If only she knew...

Angelique smiled sadly. Sooner or later Nikolai would find out about this and she would pay the price. "You should go. Pack your things and book the soonest flight to New York." She urged.

"What will happen to you?" Zoe's expression grew serious.

"I don't know." She couldn't lie. "But I will think of something. I have a running deal with the devil after all."

Chapter 24

The time was like quicksand, running out faster than she could blink.

It took every ounce of effort to pry Zoe from the integration session. If they were meant to meet again, she would answer every question. Now, however, she had to get back to the mansion before her absence had struck notice.

The looming though that it probably already has made her insides turn liquid.

Pushing those dark thoughts to the back of her head, Angelique rushed down the dark red corridors. The tingling in her spine got the small hair on her arms standing on end. You robbed the mob boss. The gnawing voice within her reminded. You stole his money. He has killed for less.

She swallowed dryly. No turning back now. If he chose to dump her corpse at the bottom of the sea, she at least knew it was for a good cause. Nikolai was vicious when angry. And this would most certainly make him angry.

Angelique rounded the corner in hurry and -

She whumped straight into something. No. Someone.

The person grunted with the collision. Two men stood short way from the exit, and she had ran head first into one of them. Losing her balance, the young woman fell straight on her butt. Damn, the landing wasn't smooth. Sharp pain rushed through her like a bullet when she caught most of her weight on her bad arm.

"Well, well..." A voice made her look up.

Her blood turned cold. She knew these men. Nikolai's goons, the very same ones he had gathered in his office to find out who had arranged the attack.

"Is the little Angel lost?" She did not like his tone. Low and menacing.

"This certainly changes things, huh." The other man grunted.

"She's just his bedroom toy." The first man stated dully, tang of disdain in his voice.

"I don't think so, Alik." The nameless man stepped closer to where she was still sitting on the ground. Angelique scurried away, but froze on the spot before she could properly stand. In a flash the man had his gun pointed at her head. "Up." He barked.

When she didn't move, he growled. "Get up or I will shoot you."

The young woman slowly shuffled onto her feet. Something told her that these men weren't really working for Nikolai. That her previous fear of his wrath was nothing compared to what they would do to her if she disobeyed.

"She'll be a dead weight." Alik glared at his companion.

"No. She is his weakness." The man cut in, sizing her up from toe. "You will be a smart girl and do as we say." It wasn't a question. It was a warning. One his gloved hands shot out, grasping her forearm in a painful hold.

On pure instinct, Angelique tugged on her arm, only to be sharply pulled against the rough man's chest. He was unpleasant through and through. His aging features wrinkled in fearsome scowl and lips formed into a sneer.

A vibe of petty gangster radiated off of the duo in waves. They would not hesitate to put a hole in her if she as much as took a step in the wrong direction.

"We have to hurry up." Alik stressed. "I don't want this whole deal going south because you picked up his whore."

Angelique grit her teeth not to say anything to that. "What the hell do you want from me-"

"Shut your pretty trap before I chose to do it." The man holding her spat, tugging on her arm harder to force her to move.

She regretted not choosing a different route. If she had gone through the club instead of backdoor nothing like this would've happened.

The gun dug into her lower back, cold metal a clear warning. "Walk." The gangster ordered, pushing the tip of his colt further into her flesh. "It would be a pity to have such pretty lil' thing paralyzed, hm?"

Now Angelique was certain that she had not only stepped on someones toes, but all out rolled a tank over them. If God was a thing, she was his least favorite creation of all time.

A quick in and out, huh. Great plan...She mused bitterly.

They forced her down the hallway. Alik moved first, alert of their surroundings, while the other man made sure she didn't skip off. One of his rough hands were digging into her bad shoulder, adding pressure whenever she glanced at door they passed. A couple of threats were mindlessly thrown in for the hell of it. A scared prisoner was ought to obey.

Alik swung open the backdoor of the club, motioning for them to go first. Angelique stumbled over her own steps with a violent shove. "Go, and don't think of doing anything funny." He warned, never fully releasing her from the gun point.

That thing could blow off any moment, putting her in wheelchair for life. If one thing was for sure, she did not trust the jerky finger on the trigger. The odd trio slipped outside the club into the dark alleyway. The perfect place to dump a body. Dreadful stench of piss, trash and vomit would mask her rotting body.

For better or worse, the two men had different plans. They lead her past the green dumpsters, pushing her further towards the street where a black car was waiting.

"Get in-" Alik was cut off mid sentence. His eyes traveled down to his stomach. Large stain of blood was soaking through his shirt. The man sunk to his knees moment later, clutching his middle section that was leaking his life source.

"Let her go." A calm, authoritative voice boomed through the alleyway.

Nikolai.

Angelique gasped. The gangster whirled around, pressing her back flush against him. The gun went to the side of her head faster than she could blink. It was like a scene from a movie. The bad guy holding the damsel in distress hostage while her hero stood tall some distance from them.

A gun with a silencer was firmly clenched in Nikolai's hand. Alik had slumped over on the ground, moaning in pain inflicted by the perfectly aimed shot. Dog stood besides his boss, his expression giving away close to nothing.

"I will blow her head off if you move." The man holding her threatened. Nikolai didn't even flinch at those words. If she didn't know better, she would think he didn't care if she got killed.

"Your attempts at my life are pitiful." Nikolai said flatly, "I shouldn't be surprised you would stomp this low." Betrayal rung clear in his voice. His silver eyes shone dangerously in the dark like ones of a wolf. "This is your last warning. Let her go."

"Fuck that." The gangster shot back. If he complied, it would hardly make Nikolai change his mind of torturing the sanity out of the man. "She's coming with me." He tugged Angelique further back, the tip of the gun pressing painfully into her temple.

Nikolai's eyes narrowed. His back straightened, and chin jutted up hauntingly. The darkness in his gaze intensified, lingering just on the edge of something crazed. If her life wouldn't be on the line, Angelique would pity the poor guy that got that look. But - oh, that's right - that poor guy still held a fucking gun at her head! No pity for him then.

"Last warning." One might've missed the subtle glance, but not Dog. He was trained properly and loyal to the fault.

Angelique felt her breath glitch in her lungs. Within seconds the trusted sidekick had a gun of his own pointed at the man holding her. She squeezed her eyes shut. This had to be it. The end of her.

A silenced, muffled thud reached her ears seconds later, followed by a strained noise emitting from the gangster's throat.

His grip loosened, and the gun he held pressed against her slid down the side of her face before cluttering down on the pavement. Her eyes peeled open when she felt suddenly pressure on her back. It pressed down at her severely. With her captor's arms having grown slack around her, she quickly grasped the chance to side step him.

The second she did, the guy went down full force. His eyes were wide open and no longer alive. Neat hole had replaced one of his eyes, oozing liquid she was too cowardly to name.

Her knees quavered. She released a shaky breath, her eyes trailing back up to the two men still standing.

The relief was short lived. When she turned to look, Nikolai was marching towards her.

And boy, was he pissed.

Chapter 25

S ilence hung heavy. Suffocating.

Not a single word was exchanged during the dense ride back to the mansion. He didn't touch or or even glance at her with those stormy eyes of his. Usually Angelique was the one avoiding his intense gaze, huddled up in the far corner. This time, she was sneaking peeks at his sharp profile.

Nikolai's thick eyebrows were furrowed and his lips turned down into a scowl. He was brooding in silence. She was certain he caught her looking, but didn't return the notion. The young woman was left feeling sick with apprehension.

He was first to get out from the car when it finally came to a grinding halt in front of the looming building. The sound of door slamming behind him got her to flinch. She was swarmed by dozen awful scenarios of what would happen once he was updated on all subtle details of how one of his men wound up stuck in his office.

I'm as good as dead.

Angelique turned her head to the ground, trying desperately to make a wallflower out of herself until she reached her room. No luck.

The second they were inside the mansion, Nikolai caught her wrist in an iron grip.

"Wait-" She didn't get to squeak as he dragged her upstairs without a word.

The noise of door slamming shut behind them made her ears ring. The bedroom was dim, their harsh breaths the only thing disturbing the silence. His massive frame leaned against the door, blocking her exit. Smokey-grey eyes stared at her coldly. He had let go of her hand, but his gaze kept her pinned.

Angelique straightened her back. There was no avoiding this. "I can explain-"

"You disobeyed." He cut her off curtly, his eyes narrowing to thin slits. "You stole from me." He added. It wasn't the sum she took that bothered him. No. It was the principle.

Like a tiger stalking its innocent prey, Nikolai closed the distance between them in two large steps. "Did you really think I wouldn't find out?"

"No." She frowned. "I knew you would." Hard to miss the man she had locked inside his office. "I promised Zoe that I would help-"

"And that give you the right to take what is not yours?" He growled. Nikolai looked seconds away from connecting his fist with her jaw. "You have forgotten your place-"

"What is my place, exactly?!" Angelique roared. Stupid courage streamed through her blood like lava. "To be your toy when you need a relief? For a moment I thought..." She paused, sucking in a deep breath. "I thought I was something more. That this meant something."

Emotions swam in his dark eyes. Her words struck. She saw the flick of change before it was masked by anger. In a fluid motion he reached out, grasping her golden hair. It wasn't painful. Not physically at least.

"It does." He admitted. "But it gives you no right to interfere with my business." He was struggling with himself. With his boiling rage.

If she was someone else, she would be laying face in dirt, counting seconds until her life would fade. He looked torn, like he had no idea what to do with her now. Caught red handed, and stubborn - she didn't regret anything that had lead her to this point.

"What are you going to do now? Punish me?" She didn't mean to taunt him. But she did. Zoe was right, she had grown up from her timid, scared self. With so little to lose, she felt brave enough to tug the devil's tail. "Are you going to kill me?"

"No." Nikolai growled as if the though alone set him on edge. He leaned closer. "I will make sure you don't ever disobey me again." His voice dropped, turning cold and malicious. His hand in her hair curled in a fist by her scalp. Now it was painful.

Angelique's eyes widened when he pressed an angry, open mouthed kiss on her lips. She moaned in protest. His tongue force its way inside her mouth, exploring. It was a dominating kiss, meant to put her in her place.

Two can play this game.

She bit down on his lower lip. Hard.

He growled in pain, which only provoked his next move. A loud rrriiippp sounded through the room. Her shirt was torn apart with a forceful jerk, falling to her feet.

This was nothing like the sensual moments they had exchanged when she was wounded. The gentle love making. Hell. This was all out battle.

It was her turn to growl when her bra was torn from her body. He was stripping her naked while still having a full suit on. Furiously, she tugged off his jacket and nearly ripped open the vest. He wasn't making the job any easier, pushing her up against the wall with enough force to make her breath catch.

His large hands grasped her ass, tugging her legs around his waist while his rough lips moved down her neck. He bit her, hard enough to leave a mark on its wake. Talking this out was out of the picture. They pulled each other under.

Nikolai's hips grind against her pelvis. He was rock hard.

Angelique clawed at his back as he propped her up against the windowsill. Their clothes fell to shreds, long forgotten. His hungry lips devoured every inch of her, his teeth nipping painfully at her hardened nipples in revenge for his bleeding bottom lip. A desperate whine slipped past her lips.

The tension between them built up until neither could take it anymore. Her thighs were forced open, Nikolai settling between them. He assessed her with eyes so hot they could melt her.

Then, without a warning he set the thick tip of his erection against her entrance and his hips slammed against her.

Mercilessly, he pounded inside her. His moves were angry, rough - the essence of raw power. She trembled beneath him, her back pressing against the cold glass of the window with no regard of who might see them from the backyard.

Nikolai sounded like a vicious beast claiming what was his. Snarling and growling against her neck. No amount of scratching, biting or hair pulling could slow him down. In fact, it had the opposite effect. Every time her nails racked against his muscular back, he would deepen his thrusts.

Her muscles clenched around him. But just as Angelique was about to tip over the edge, he flipped them over. Both of her hands settled on the cold glass.

"I want you to watch yourself come undone." He whispered gruffly into her ear, biting her earlobe. She was too breathless to respond. He didn't need her to. Nikolai thrust back inside her. Her eyes rolled shut.

"Watch!" He ordered, grasping her blond hair to have her head tilting back. She obeyed. Angelique watched their reflection as Nikolai drove himself inside her. Unconsciously she moaned out his name over and over again. Orgasm shook her body, making her mind go blank.

Nikolai wasn't far off. The second the waves of pleasure subsided, he was pulling out, something warm spilling across her lower back. He grunted with the powerful sensation.

When she fully came to, she was slumped against the windowsill, exhausted. Nikolai leaned over her, stroking his fingers through her long hair.

"There is your punishment." She could hear the satisfied smirk in his voice. "Next time you pull a stunt like that," He grasped her throat from behind, pulling her flush against him with little care of how well she could breath. "I will make sure you can't walk for a week when I'm done."

Chapter 26

"Breakfast is ready." Irina's cheerful voice cut through the dark room. Delicious smell filled the air. Beacon with eggs. Her stomach growled, her head lifting lazily from the fluffy pillow.

Two days later, she still felt sore. Nikolai was true to his word. The night of her 'punishment' made her legs quiver even now. He took her roughly over and over again. Against the wall, on the floor, on bed and even followed her in the shower for another round. When she collapsed from pure exhaustion, he reminded her that she could go once more until her insides were aching.

Her entire body was littered with love bites.He had claimed every inch of her with his lips, teeth and firm touch. The scent of his cologne lingered on the sheets. She hadn't noticed when he left, but for some reason her heart ached that she didn't wake up with his warmth around her.

"Thank you." Angelique murmured, pushing all those thoughts at the back of her head.

Irina gave her a knowing grin. "Don't mention it. I heard what happened." Her expression grew serious. "Did you really do it?" Clearly, she was referring to stealing from Nikolai.

"I did." There was no point lying. "I had to help a friend."

"I heard one of the guards complaining that you locked him in." Irina arranged food on a silver platter as she spoke. "It's very brave of you."

"You mean stupid?"

"Maybe a little." The maid chuckled, settling the food in Angelique's lap with a newspaper on the side. "No one else would've gotten away with it. You really are special."

Sudden warmth spread across her cheeks. For some reason hearing that she was special to Nikolai made her heart sing. "I don't know about that."

"Oh come on. Don't pretend, you know you are. Between us girls..." Irina leaned in as if she was about to reveal a top secret. "Nikolai was grinning like a school boy at his laptop when I brought him coffee this morning. I have never seen him smile like that."

Angelique was sure her face was fifty shades of red at this point. "Maybe he landed a good business deal or something."

"Uh-huh." Irina gave her an odd look that nearly screamed - You know he landed something else. "I'll leave you to your breakfast. Oh, and, when you're done, the successful business lion wants you in his office." She winked playfully, scurrying out from the room before Angelique could say another word.

My God...

She slumped back into the sheets, wide smile playing on her lips. Her life was nothing like it had been before she met Nikolai, but for the first time in long, she felt happy again. This was entirely different kind of happiness ,and she embraced it despite the mixed feelings. It felt good.

Butterflies danced in her stomach. Idly, she found herself thinking what to wear after breakfast. Nikolai loved to see her in white. Maybe she could wear a summer dress.

Angelique took the first bite from the divine tasting breakfast when the headline of the newspaper caught her eye.

A man found dead in house fire!

Color drained from her face. Shakily, her finger unfolded the newspaper. Large picture of burning house was printed on the first page. Picture of her house.

Her stomach twisted into knots.

Man found dead....

House fire...

An accident...

Her head begun to spin, the words echoing through her mind over and over again.

"No.." She chocked out. Violent sobs wrecked her body. The breakfast was long forgotten. The sight of it alone made her want to vomit. Tears dripped down on the pages. The lines blurred until she couldn't read any further.

Dad! No!

Then it clicked.

Cold sweat broke out on her skin. The shock made it hard to breath. There was only one person capable of doing something like this. Only he could've done it.

Her hands went into her hair, gripping hard against the blond locks. Desperation, hatred, blind rage, sorrow - all those awful emotions rushed through like a tsunami.

You naive fool...

For a moment she thought that she actually meant something to him. The blissful moment of peace shuttered, cold realization settling in her gut. He killed her father.

He killed him! I defied him and he is punishing me again. He's a monster. A fucking monster! And I can't escape him.

Escape. The words lingered in the back of her head. There was only one way out for her.

Angelique forced herself out from the bed, newspaper clutched in one hand. The spark in her eyes was replaced by emptiness. She wanted to look into his eyes, let him see what he had done.

This was on him.He wanted to break her and he had succeeded.

Nikolai was sitting at his desk when she entered his office. The grey eyes lifted from glowing screen of his laptop. The hardened exterior dissipated somewhat when he saw her. His lips parted to greet her-

"You monster." She cut him off. Her voice was cold...empty.

A deep frown formed on his handsome face at the sight of her tears. She tossed the newspaper at him, letting it drop atop his desk.

"You monster." The young woman repeated dully. "This is on you. Dale...my dad...things you did to Amanda and me." She choked out the words, forcing them past her lips. "It's all on you. To think that for a moment I-" Another sob shook her body. "I thought you might have changed. That things could be different....I was such a fool. You are a fucking monster after all!"

Angelique didn't wait for his reaction. She stormed out from his office.

"Angel!" Nikolai's roar echoed down the hall, followed by the heavy stomp of his rushing footsteps.

Run! Faster! The voice in her head urged, and she obeyed. The young woman sprinted down the waving corridor and down the countless steps towards the grand entrance.

"Angelique!" Nikolai was hot on her heels. "Stop!" He ordered.

She did not listen. Instead she forced herself to go faster. He was gaining on her. If he caught her, she would be his trapped angel for forever, forced to watch all her loved ones die, hunted down one by one just to remind her where she belonged.

Faster!

Adrenaline rushed through her veins like electricity. She burst through the double-side door and shambled down the stairs towards line of neatly parked cars, always at the ready to run the devil's errands.

"Hey!" One of the drivers lingering around yelled when she slipped into the car. "Stop-" She did not linger to listen, pressing the 'start' button. The engine roared to life just as Nikolai ripped open the driver's side door.

"Angel-" He reached for her, and she slammed on the gas pedal. The Mercedes lurched forwards, the door still hanging ajar. The tires dug through the lawn, leaving muddy tracks in their wake.

Her attention was fixed on large metallic gate. Guards standing by shuffled to have them closed as quickly as possible. The speed escalated. They were Nikolai's loyal hounds. And clearly unaware of how desperate she was.

One of the guards jumped in front of the car, thinking she would hit the breaks.

Wrong.

Angelique squeezed her eyes shut when the front of the car collided with the body. The man crashed in the windshield and rolled across the vehicle. Thick red blood was smeared across the glass and the dull thud of the crash was like a gunshot to her ears. Still, she couldn't stop. Not now. Not ever.

The car zinged past the guards through the small opening in the gate. Some of it caught the sides of the Mercedes, metal clashing against metal and completely tearing off the driver side door. Through the cracks in the glass, the blood and her own tears, she could barely see anything.

Faster! The voice urged again.

She didn't have to look to know she was being tailed. Wind whipped at her skin, howling past her with the brutal speed. Her small hands clutched the wheel in an iron grip. The speedometer jumped when she switched gear.

120...130...140...

Faster! faster!

A sporty BMW was closing in on her damaged Mercedes, headlights blinking in warning. It wasn't the only car chasing her. She could see a couple more at further distance, some taking turns to block her road later on. Shit!

Fear clawed at her insides like a beast. She couldn't escape them. Not unless...

Her eyes flicked to the side. Ominous woods were slowly thinning and soon she was speeding across a bridge.

The BMW honked, its metallic body gaining speed to cut her off before she reached the end of the bridge. The car slid into the line besides her, one of the tinted windows rolling down. Nikolai's stormy grey eyes met her own. He yelled something, but all she could hear was the howling of the wind.

"This is on you." Angelique mouthed.

His eyes widened in horror and then-

She whipped the wheel to the side. The Mercedes crashed full-force into the banister. The sheer power of the collision mixed with the speed sent the car flying. Raging water of river underneath would be her death bed. She saw it clear as day and smiled.

The Angel had spread its wings and had escaped the devil's trap.

She was free.

Chapter 27

Nikolai.

The floor of the old warehouse was damp and cold. Air smelled like mold and blood. His blood. Nikolai felt it pooling around his frame. Sometime around now his father would yell for him to man up. You got hurt? So what?

His eyes closed. For once he was in peace with his fate. Calm and silent death. It was far better than what would come otherwise. He just had to wait until he bled out. A fifteen-year-old could certainly find himself in a far better situation, but he wasn't just a regular teenager. He was next in line to lead an Empire of crime and violence.

Yeah, death did sound good.

Bang! Crash!

"Danny! You stupid, be silent!" A distant, childish voice whisper-yelled. It clearly belonged to a young boy. "We shouldn't be here."

"Shut up. Are you a coward? It's going to be fine!" Another, equally young voice claimed.

"This is scary." A female voice joined the conversation. "I don't like this place."

"Are you scared of ghosts, Angelique?" The brash boy quipped.

"N-no. I just don't like it here." The girl protested. Their voices were nearing.

Nikolai stifled an annoyed groan. Fucking hell, he couldn't even die without being bothered, by kids no less. Maybe if he laid there silently they wouldn't find-

"Oh my god!" One of the boys suddenly yelled.

No rest for the wicked. Nikolai kept his eyes closed, very much aware of three young kids ogling his bleeding form from a corner.

"Let's get out of here!" The other boy insisted, sounding panicked.

"What!? We can't just leave him like this!" The girl protested.

"Whatever. I am not staying!" The two boys shuffled away in hurry.

Smart thing to do, Nikolai noted. But one of the group remained standing still. The girl had stayed behind. Finally the curiosity got the best of him. He peered at her though his lashes, getting a glimpse of her delicate horror-filled face, her large doe-like eyes, and the most striking feature of all - her golden hair.

The girl wasn't a day older than seven, maybe eight. She looked like an angel - so pure and innocent, it felt wrong to be in her presents. He deserved to die on this cold floor - alone.

"Are you awake?" She questioned in a soft voice, slowly approaching.

Nikolai felt an urge to yell at her - to tell her to get lost like her friends did. But he remained silent, watching her through squinted eyes.

Hesitantly, she knelt down besides him. The girl gasped in shock when she saw the large wound that split open his chest all the way down to his torso. "We need to call an ambulance-"

"No." Nikolai rasped. His voice was rough for a teenager and harsh enough to make her flinch. That's it.If he scared her away he could die in peace. "Go away." He ordered, failing to sound demanding.

This time it was her turn to say no. "I won't do that. I can't leave you here." The angelic girl removed her jacket, pressing it against his open wound.

Nikolai winced. "I don't need your help."

"You look like you do."

Damn, she's stubborn.

"Leave." He demanded again.

"No." She refused.

"If you won't leave me, I will hurt you." The boy threatened lamely.

"Hold up, I will get you some bandages." The girl right up ignored him. Briskly, she stood up. "Don't go anywhere!" She ordered fiercely for an eight-year-old.

Nikolai scoffed. As if I could. He watched the girl scurry away. She had left her jacket on him, letting it soak with his blood. It was warm, like her. He let his eyes drop close, certain she wouldn't return. No one would return for someone like me. He though bitterly, not really feeling too successful. He had scared her away, but it did not feel good.

Whatever. You're not meant to feel good. You're meant to die.

To his utter shock, the girl returned half an hour later with a first aid kit and some food. He was shaken from his slumber by her slender fingers undoing his shirt.

"This is awful. Who did this to you?" The girl questioned, her cornflower blue eyes sad. "My name is Angelique by the way. What's your name?"

Nikolai didn't respond, still shellshocked by her return.

"Fine, you don't have to tell me." She grumbled, fumbling with a piece of gauze. "Can you at least sit up?"

He did as told, well, tried. The pain and exhaustion made him slump right back against the cold ground. "Why are you doing this?" He grit out, attempting once more to prop himself up. This time he succeeded somewhat.

Angelique frowned as if the answer was obvious. "I can't let you bleed out." She cleaned his wound and wrapped a gauze around his torso. Nikolai's body was littered with wounds and adorned a couple of tattoos. He saw it in her eyes, she wanted to ask what they meant, but instead concentrated on the task.

It was a sloppy work of a eight year old, but he couldn't wish for more. She had him lay on a thick blanket she had brought and eat a sandwich. What an odd girl.

"There. You're set." She announced proudly once she had Nikolai tucked in and fed. "I will come back tomorrow to change the bandages and bring you food."

Silently the boy watched her collect her things. He didn't utter a word as she walked out.

Angelique kept her word. For the following week, she treated his dressings and brought him food. Even chocolate. Everyday she revealed something new about herself. Apparently she liked dancing and wanted to become a dancer when she grew up. She also liked sweets and butterflies.

He got a feeling that she didn't have anyone to talk to back at home. Nikolai pitied her that he was the best company the sunshine of a girl had. A petty son of a gang lord.

Still, he listened, and a couple of times felt compelled to reveal a thing or two about himself as well.

A week later, she had him nursed back to health to the point where he could stand and change his own dressings. The young girl was too kind to him. He couldn't help getting attached to her. She was light to his darkness. So pure and innocent - like a gulp of fresh air.

Sadly, he couldn't stay hiding in the warehouse for forever. He was alive and well, and full of scalding anger. Those who wronged him - his own family - would pay the price.

"What do you mean, you have to go?" Angelique questioned when he revealed that he was going to leave the warehouse.

"I can't hide here for forever, Angel." Nikolai couldn't stand the sad look in her eyes. "But I tell you what, let's make a promise."

"A promise?" She lit up. "Like a pinky promise?"

He chuckled. "Something like that." Slowly, he stretched out his hand, offering her his pinky. "I promise that I will forever be yours. No matter what. Even if we don't ever meet again, you have a part of my soul." He felt his cheeks flame at such cheesy words, even if he meant every single one of them.

Angelique beamed, wrapping her much smaller pinky around his. "Then I promise that I will forever be yours, and you will always have a piece of my soul." She locked her finger around his. "Cross my heart and hope to die!"

His heart melted then and there. She was just a kid, he knew it. But when she would grow up, she would kill men with a single glance, he was certain.

Nikolai reached out, pulling into a firm hug. Their parting embrace. "Cross my heart and hope to die..." He repeated after her, squeezing her tighter against him.

If we ever meet again...I won't ever let you go, my Angel.

Chapter 28

Angelique

Death is not supposed to be painful. It's peaceful darkness that embraces you. It makes you forget. But she remembered everything - the old house with leaking ceiling she grew up in, the warmth of sun against her skin, the thick grey clouds of stormy days and...the eyes in color of steel.

Those eyes that reminded her of rain after scalding hot summer day. They stared back at her from depths of her memory, sharp, unyielding and sad.

And then there was the pain, ever-present and very real. She felt it all over.

Something was beeping steadily in distance. The sound became louder, disturbing the brittle images she had been admiring in her head. It pulled her to the surface.

Angelique felt a jolt like electricity. It shook her entire body and made her eyes open to a bright room. The searing light was painful and oddly welcome. White ceiling, white walls, white everything.

Her chest raised and fell. Every breath was painful like her lungs had been stabbed by thousand knives. But it did not matter. She was breathing. Oxygen flowed into her system and the blinding light subsided somewhat.

A pale hospital ward greeted her blurry vision.

I'm alive...

Angelique felt something squeeze her hand assuringly as if to confirm her idle thought. Her blue eyes focused on the source of the warm touch. A large carouse hand held her own, long tattooed fingers intertwined with hers.

Messy walnut color hair cascaded down the man's rugged features. He was slumped over in an uncomfortable metallic chair besides the hospital bed, fast asleep.

Inwardly, she felt the need to flinch, pull her hand away, but it remained in place, cradled by a familiar touch. Nikolai always looked peaceful in his sleep, like no sins he had committed ever haunted him. This time was different. His eyebrows were creased into a deep frown. He looked tired, like he had been stuck by her side the entire time.

The stubble on his face teetered on edge of beard and his usually well groomed hair were wild and unkempt. The facade had cracked and underneath she saw...

"You're that boy..." Angelique murmured coarsely. She saw the boy she had helped all those years ago - a boy with dark past and sad, stormy eyes. A memory buried so deep she hadn't come to realize who he was. Until now.

Nikolai stirred. Her whisper had been a silent croak. It was a miracle he had heard her. His eyes opened, dull grey and red-rimmed. The man lifted his head, moving slowly as if it weighed a ton. "Angel." The groggy rasp in his voice sent a jolt of electricity through her. It sounded cracked like he hadn't spoken in days. "You're awake." he stated in near disbelief.

There were so many things she wanted to ask, to scream at him even, but all that came out was a pained moan. Her entire body was battered. Her other arm sported a massive gypsum. The white mass was wrapped from her wrist up to her elbow. She couldn't move her body. The pain was too much despite the medication she was on.

"You broke three ribs and your arm. You had two surgeries to stop internal bleeding." Nikolai explained. "They kept you in medicine infused coma."

"For how long?"

"Two weeks."

Her eyes closed and she sucked in a breath. Last thing she remembered was the impact of the car crashing into the raging river. She was not supposed to survive that. "How did I..."

"I pulled you out from the water."

Angelique forced her eyes open. He was looking at her with pained gaze, like she had ripped out a part of his soul and crushed it. "I didn't kill your father."

"Don't-" She couldn't stand listening to this. It would make it real - the hospital, her injuries, and the fact that she was now all alone. The only person at her bedside was the one that put her there in the first place. It was all his fault.

"I am many things but not a liar."

She did not want to listen. A part of her was hoping he was a liar. But his stormy grey eyes rung truth.

"Police suspect it was an accident. He fell asleep drunk and dropped a burning cigarette."

The cold hearted truth poured over her head. It did sound like her father could've done something like that. Her pitiful dad had met pitiful end. She felt tears prick her eyes.

"I wish it wouldn't be the first thing you heard after waking up." Nikolai whispered. "I brought you to it. The suicide attempt." He looked deep into her teary eyes. "I ruined you."

"Wasn't that your goal?"

"No." His jaw clenched. "I wanted you to be mine. Like you promised..."

"I remember." Angelique had to clear her throat not to choke. "You're that boy from warehouse. You never told me your name."

Nikolai stared down at her, tense. "I never expected to see you again." He confessed. "I kept our promise locked away. I hoped we wouldn't meet again. Then you would see the monster I have become. But..." He trailed off. "But then you showed up at my club. Pure and innocent like the day I first saw you. I was so angry."

"Why?" Her voice shook.

"Because you didn't remember. I was so fucking mad, I wanted to destroy you. That promise meant everything to me, and you..." He looked down, fists clenched. "You forgot."

Angelique was speechless. He looked so sad, desperate almost. She couldn't deny the holes in her memory, self created at that. For the longest time she fought to forget the darkest parts of her childhood. Her mom died when she was eight, her father drunk himself stupid every evening. The young woman had wanted to forget it all, and had succeeded. Her mind was a prison containing all the memories she kept locked away to keep herself sane.

"I hurt you." Nikolai continued. For the longest time she thought he hated her, but the look in his eyes screamed that he hated himself not her. "I'm as fucked up as they get. I drove the woman I love towards destruction."

Love....

The words echoed through her head like a gunshot.

"I loved you since that day in the warehouse...." He gripped his hair. "But I fucked it all up because I wanted you all for myself, but your spirit was too free to tame. I hurt you because I was jealous. And I can't change that."

She drew in a deep breath. "You can't change...even for me?" Angelique tried to deny the part of her that had become attracted to him. Perhaps she was mentally ill. Perhaps he had made her so sick that she couldn't leave him. For a long time, she had known that she loved him as well. It was taboo and fucked up. He was a monster, and she was his Angel.

Nikolai's fingers intertwined with her own. "I have always been the worst this world has produced. I will always be..." He swallowed. "A monster."

Angelique looked down at their locked hands. His warmth, his scent, the sorrowful grey eyes, it all made her heart clench in pain. "Quit."

"I can't."

"Quit the mafia. For me..." She looked into his hardened eyes. He didn't have to respond, she saw it in his gaze - he would never quit. Not even for her.

"I can't keep our promise." Her voice broke, single tear trickling down her cheek. "I can't keep it unless you quit."

The muscles in his jaw ticked. "I know." He refused to look at her. "I was never the man for you. I knew that from the start." He released her hands, his warmth replaced by the chilly air.

"Don't-"

"We had a deal." His voice was cold even if his eyes told story of pain and suffering. "And you did your part." Nikolai stood up from the chair. He leaned over her, taking in her features one last time.

"Why does it seem like you're saying goodbye?" Angelique choked out. Tears kept streaming down her cheeks.

"Because I am." Nikolai wiped away her tears. He pressed a gentle, lingering kiss to her forehead.

"You're free, Angelique."

Epilogue

2 years later.

New York - Broadway.

Spotlights. Applause. She stared into the dark crowd from the stage. Fellow dancers fell into line besides her to bow for the public. Clapping of hands and a couple of cheers echoed through the auditorium in waves. The performers bent their heads, some accepting flowers from their fans.

Her dream had come true. The yellow roses a ten year old girl pressed into her arms reminded her of how far she had come since the day in the hospital.

Angelique never saw him again. Even now, she looked at the crowd in naive hope catch a glimpse of those stormy grays.

He had ensured she recovered, even sent her money when she moved to New York a month later. She refused to accept a single cent. Nikolai had made his choice that day. Power over love.

Hurt, miserable and heartbroken, she left behind her old life to start over. But even then, no man had concurred her heart. It would forever belong to him - her kidnapper and lover. She would forever be his angel, he would forever be the monster that selfishly stole away her soul.

"That was amazing." A familiar voice cheered the second dancers got off the stage. Zoe stood on the side, holding a red-haired boy to her hip. Toby looked like a male, baby version of his mother. Big green eyes, red hair - born a charmer. Whoever was the father, he got the best features. All future ladies had to be careful.

"I thought you wouldn't make it." Angelique beamed, pulling her friend into a tight hug.

"Ew. You're sweaty."

"Sorry - did you miss the two hours of me dancing my ass off?" She retorted playfully.

Zoe grinned. "How could I miss that. Maybe you suck at stripping, but you pulled quite a number there. You have a talent."

"Hello. This is Broadway. I wouldn't be here if I didn't have talent. And you wouldn't be here if I wasn't one of the performers."

"Since when are you so cocky?" Zoe chuckled, adjusting slightly cranky Toby in her arms.

"You mean powerful, confident young woman?" Angelique joked, her lips easing into a light-hearted smile.

"Huh. The same." The red head rolled her eyes. "Toby is getting tired. I know you wanted to grab a coffee-"

"It's quite alright. Go home, you need the rest. I am glad you could make it." She assured.

"How could I not? After everything you did for me this is the least I could do."

"You have to stop bringing that up every time we meet."

Truth was, Zoe had returned the favor when Angelique first came to New York. They grew closer than ever, helped each other through hard times. Let it be finding a job or going to physiotherapy after the car crash, or raising Toby - they stuck together.

Angelique still mourned her father's death. Those were bad days, but she was never alone with them. Amanda was there. Zoe was there. She had friends and new life, without the one person she wished to have a new life with....

Saying quick goodbye to the lucky mother and her adorable son, she made her way to the changing rooms. Next big act was on Wednesday, which gave her plenty of time to rest. Amanda had suggested dating, but the thought alone made her stomach twist in knots.

"Wanna join us for a drink?" One of the fellow dancers asked as they left through the staff exit.

"No thanks. I'm a bit tired. I will go home." Angelique refused politely, adjusting the duffle bag over her shoulder.

"Suit yourself. Have a great night!"

She waved to her colleagues while fishing out her headphones from the massive mess that was her bag. The young woman was about to give up when the world came to a crashing halt with a single word. A single male voice.

"Angel."

The bag fell onto the ground. Her eyes widened. Every nerve in her body stood at end. No..that couldn't possibly be...She swiveled around, and her heart nearly stopped. Deep grey eyes stared back at her.

Nikolai was leaning against the hood of a black car, dressed in his signature black suit. His hair were shorter, slicked back neatly, and the stubble trimmed to a five o'clock shadow. The intensity in his gaze hadn't changed. The grey orbs carried the same sharpness she had fallen for so helplessly.

"You're more beautiful than I remember..." He whispered, slowly approaching her.

""What...why?" Angelique stammered. She couldn't put together a single sentence, shocked.

"I quit."

Her eyes widened.

"It took time. But I quit....for you...and for myself..." Hesitantly, he reached out to caress her blond hair. "I can't ask you to be with me. You would never be safe. But I had to see you again. These two years...I couldn't stop thinking about you. Every day and every night, I wished you were besides me." A slow smile unfurled on his lips. "You've gotten so far. I'm glad to see you doing well."

The blur of emotions made her tremble. Without thinking, she threw her arms around him. "You quit." Her voice shook.

Nikolai wrapped his arms around her tightly. "I did."

"What are you gonna do now?"

"I don't know. I was raised to be a vile man. I have to find a new purpose." He whispered in her hair, resting his cheek against the crown of her head.

"You say that I will be in danger if I stay with you, but I feel the most at ease right now than I've been in two years." Angelique murmured, pulling back slightly to look into his eyes. "I want to be with you."

"Even after everything I did?"

"I still haven't forgiven you fully..." She admitted. "Someday, I will."

Nikolai caressed her cheek, resting his forehead against her own. "This is how it was supposed to be."

"What exactly?"

"Our reunion. It was supposed to be like this, not the shit-show from two years ago."

She chuckled softly. "Yeah." Her eyes drifted close. "I kept my promise. You have part of my soul, no one else can have it but you."

Nikolai tightened his grip on her. "And you have my soul. Only you, Angelique." He tilted up her chin. "Look at me."

She did. His eyes were full of emotion. "Forgive me. I can't promise to be a good man, but I will try every day to become better, to keep the darkness at bay. Will you..." He trailed off. "I hope one day, you will find it in you to forgive me."

"Nikolai, I-" Angelique felt tears raising forth. She didn't hold them back, letting him wipe them away. "I love you."

"I have always loved you, Angel." He admitted, leaning to lock their lips in a deep kiss. It was filled with passion, love and longing so strong, her legs nearly gave out.

"One day, I will be a man worthy of your love. That's my new promise to you."

"And I promise to be there for you every step at the way."

Angelique pulled him into a deep kiss. She was his angel, and he was the monster that stole her heart - man of darkness, that she showed the light to. Their love was taboo, something that should't exist, but it was real, burning....and strong.